Lovers and Lace

DELCINIA DIARIES BOOK ONE

DANIA VOSS

DANIA VOSS

Edited by Kay Springsteen

Formatting by Laura M. Baird

Cover Design by Lynn Spangler

Visit Dania's website at https://www.daniavoss.com

Contents

About Lovers and Lace

Is a love that burns too brightly at the start, destined to combust in the end?

Olivia Wilson and Sergio Martinez fell hard and fast the day they met. But with twenty-year-old Olivia about to embark on a modeling career with Delcinia, a luxury lingerie brand and the older

Sergio pressured to devote time to his family's struggling international clothing company Martinez Designs, they aren't given a chance.

Until they reunite nine years later.

When Olivia's determination to become a driving force behind the Delcinia brand is threatened, Sergio emerges as the unlikely person who can salvage her plans, much to her dismay.

Can these two keep it professional and join forces for the sake of the company or will the chemistry that continues to sizzle between them send them both up in flames?

Chapter One

February

Olivia Wilson couldn't believe she had screwed up her future before it had even begun. Having not been able to get much sleep from being wound up after the Fashion Week Kickoff Party the night before, it had been dreadfully late by the time she'd gotten a few hours of precious sleep. Now it was Friday afternoon, mere hours before the Delcinia lingerie fashion show was due to begin, and she was scrambling to get herself together – on time. Why had she thought she could pull this off?

Olivia had wanted to be *early*. Make a good impression to her new employers, Henry and Vera Delair, founders of Delcinia, an American made, premier luxury lingerie brand. Henry and Vera had sought Olivia out on her family's dairy farm in Orrville, Ohio after seeing her in a local commercial for their super premium ice cream shop. The Delairs had been in town for a friend's wedding, and after seeing her, *knew* Olivia needed to be a member of the Delcinia family.

Not just *any* member of the Delcinia family, oh no. Olivia had been taking business classes, intending to earn her MBA. She'd never cared much for being considered a pretty face and had business plans outside of the family's Wilson Dairy. Thankful she had her parents' support.

So, after much discussion about Olivia's plans and ambitions for the future, sitting on a blanket in the pasture with her pet cow Betsy, Henry and Vera had offered Olivia the position of lead Delcinia Darling, the new face of the brand, with plans to bring her off the runway when the time came. She would become part of Delcinia's management team, with a possible investment interest in the company if everything went according to plan, after she'd earned her MBA.

And now here she was, a stupid, overconfident twenty-year-old, who couldn't even arrive to her first event on time, expecting the world from the Delairs. Olivia should just go back to Ohio, where she belonged. What had she been thinking?

"Liv, I wish you had let us, or at least me, be there with you today. I would have made sure you were up in time," her mother said, trying to be helpful, and failing miserably.

Olivia glared at her cell phone on the bathroom marble vanity countertop. The Delairs had put her up at the Grand Walhstrom Hotel in Manhattan. She'd never been anywhere so fancy before.

"Mama! I'd be even *more* nervous if any of you were here. I assured the Delairs I was mature enough to represent their company, now I have to prove it. Although I'm not off to a great start, but at least I gave myself some leeway for time." Olivia tossed a few essentials in a small backpack she was bringing with her to Lincoln Center and pulled her golden blonde locks up into a loose ponytail. She'd been instructed not to wear any makeup, not that she wore much on the farm anyway. She wore a simple pair of jeans and a blue T-shirt, a shade similar to her eye color.

"It's going to be fine. Just calm down and have the lobby call you a cab. Everything's going to be fine. I promise. It's going to be an amazing day. You'll see," her mother assured.

The warmth of her mother's love flowed through Olivia, and she calmed down just a bit. "Thanks, Mama. And don't worry, I'll make all of you proud today." The pressure to make her family and Orrville proud weighed heavily on her. She *couldn't* mess this up.

"You've already done that, honey. Long before signing with Delcinia. Seize every opportunity that comes your way from this new chapter of your life and make all your dreams come true."

That was her intention, but tears threatened. Olivia couldn't have red, swollen eyes, not before her first runway show. She inhaled deeply, trying to center herself.

"Thank you, Mama. That's exactly what I intend to do."

Olivia raced to the hotel lobby desk after a quick goodbye to her mother and enduring what had to have been the slowest elevator ride in history. She was in near full-on panic until she reached the lobby desk. Stunned stupid by the most handsome man she'd ever seen before, she stared at him like a fool. Why couldn't she ger her act together today?

Dark wavy hair, perfectly coiffed. Neatly trimmed goatee. Deep brown, soulful eyes stared right back at her, then began a slow stroll down her body. Heat pooled in her stomach and radiated outward under his sensual gaze.

Dressed to the nines in what Olivia suspected was a designer navy blue suit, the gorgeous man, perhaps Hispanic but light skinned, had been chatting up the hotel staff behind the customer service counter as she'd arrived.

Olivia mentally shook herself. She didn't have time to concern herself with the handsome stranger as much as she might have wanted to. And she wanted to. She wondered for a moment if he was a model himself, as he carried himself with style, elegance, and confidence.

No matter. Olivia had things to do and places to be. "Excuse me. I'm terribly late and I need to get to Lincoln Center. I'm in the Delcinia lingerie fashion show. Can I ask you to call a cab for me please?" Olivia directed her question to the older, refined woman without a name tag. She gave Olivia the impression that she was in charge.

The woman's warm smile reminded Olivia of her mother's and that eased her anxiety some. Everything was going to be all right, just as Olivia's mother had promised. She'd make sure of it.

Sergio Martinez stood dumbstruck and mute as the blonde-haired angel with full kissable lips who had practically floated from the elevator banks to the customer service counter asked his mother Justine Walhstrom to call her a cab to Lincoln Center. The beautiful creature before him would be gliding down the runway for Delcinia wearing the finest lingerie.

She was obviously young, possibly in her late teens, but heaven help him. The image of her walking the runway in the finest silks, satins, and lace made Sergio's heart gallop against his ribs. What he wouldn't have given to attend Delcinia's show that afternoon, but Sergio was expected to attend the Martinez Designs show, the international women's clothing company owned by the Colombian side of his family. The Walhstrom hotel, resort, and real estate empire was owned by the American side.

Grinning like an idiot, Sergio remained silent, not listening closely, as his mother and the blonde beauty discussed her transportation to Lincoln Center. When had he ever been rendered speechless when it came to a woman? Simple answer. Never. Until now.

He jerked his head toward his mother when he heard his name called and raised a brow.

Sergio's mother smiled brightly at him with a gleam in her eyes. "I was just telling Olivia you should take the car and bring her to Lincoln Center."

His mother as his wing man? It was a first, but he'd take it. Except for one important detail she must have overlooked.

"Don't worry, I'm attending the Martinez Designs show anyway. It'll be fine," his mother assured him and winked. It wasn't his mother he was concerned about though.

Olivia's face flushed and her eyes widened. Did she find him attractive? Did Sergio want her to? Yes, he most certainly did.

Olivia smiled nervously and shook her head. "I appreciate the offer, but I'm new in town and to Delcinia. I think it would be best if you called me a cab or an Uber, please."

Sergio commended her for preferring to play it safe, but she had nothing to fear from him or his family. "Our family knows Vera and Henry Delair. You're perfectly safe accepting a ride from us."

He observed Olivia closely as she considered his statement. Hopeful she'd accept their help getting to Lincoln Center. Willing to beg if he had to. What was *wrong* with him? Sergio *never* begged.

Olivia pulled out her cell phone, turned her back to them and stepped away, creating some distance between them. A smile tugged on his lips when he heard Olivia admit to Vera that she thought he was *very* handsome. His mother grinned at him from ear to ear. She was most likely already planning their wedding. He must have gone insane as the thought didn't bother him in the least.

Suddenly Olivia turned back around and approached them holding her phone out. "Okay Vera, you're on speaker."

"Sergio dear, how are you? It's been much too long," Vera said, amusement lacing her voice.

"I know it has, but I'm well. Mom's here too."

"Justine! That settles it. Allegra's in town for Fashion Week and will be at our show. Let's do brunch on Sunday if you're free. And Olivia, you should join us since we'll be apartment hunting for you anyway."

"It's a date. Olivia? Please say you'll join us?" his mother asked, her smile warm and inviting.

"Allegra Vanetti, as in Editor-in-Chief of Sophisto Moda magazine?" Olivia's lips curved up in a sweet smile that made Sergio's breath hitch.

"The one and only. She's going to love you. Please say you'll join us," Vera insisted.

Olivia glanced at him, her smile even brighter and her blue eyes twinkling. "Yes, of course. Thank you for including me." She squeaked with glee.

The ladies quickly made their plans, Olivia an obvious fan girl of the illustrious Allegra Vanetti.

He couldn't blame her. Allegra had been an international supermodel years ago, before taking over for her grandmother at Sophisto Moda. Her family owned the international publishing and mass media empire Vanetti Global Media, founded in 1925. Allegra was a huge fashion influencer in Italy and throughout Europe and had made a name for herself in the U.S. She was regarded as one of the most influential figures in fashion.

Allegra was also Sergio's former lover from several years back. Their brief "relationship" had ended amicably, and they'd remained close friends.

Sergio quickly ushered Olivia outside to his mother's white Rolls-Royce Phantom after the women had finished making their Sunday brunch plans. The February air was brisk, and he doubted Olivia's heavily lined denim jacket would keep her warm for long. The interior of the car was warm and cozy.

"You're sure we'll get there in time?" Olivia asked, her smile never dimming as she glanced around the car's interior in awe.

Sergio wished she had sat closer to him but wasn't going to push. They'd only just met, and she was young. He shouldn't have even contemplated pursuing her, considering there had to be at least a ten-year age gap between them, but he was unable to resist.

"You're going to be rather early. These shows normally begin fifteen to thirty minutes late. We'll be there in plenty of time for you to get ready. You can relax and enjoy the ride. You said you're new in town. Where are you from?" Sergio needed to know everything about her.

When Olivia focused her sparkling blues on him, his heart tripped. Shit, he was utterly enchanted by the golden-haired goddess.

She shrugged and offered a warm smile. "I'm from Orrville, Ohio. My family owns the Wilson Dairy Company. We manufacture the very best hormone free, least processed, preservative free milk products and super premium ice cream on the market."

So, she was a farmer's daughter? Why did that make her even more appealing to Sergio?

"Were you at Grand Walhstrom visiting your mother at work? And she has a Rolls-Royce? Is she the hotel manager?"

She was adorable. He knew they paid the hotel and resort staff well, but not enough for that kind of luxury.

"My mother's side of the family owns the Walhstrom chain of hotels and resorts as well as a vast real estate portfolio. Her name is Justine Walhstrom. My father's side of the family owns Martinez Designs. My Aunt Silvia and my father started the company in Bogotá. He and my mother met when Walhstrom's was expanding in Colombia." When worry marred Olivia's lovely face, Sergio wondered if he'd scared her. His family's wealth could be intimidating to some.

"Wow. Well...Wilson Dairy is on track to become a billion-dollar company soon." Olivia announced proudly.

Sergio didn't doubt it. Wilson Dairy's milk and ice cream were exceptional. Olivia should be proud of her family's success. Although he understood why she accepted a position as a Delcinia Darling, but he wondered why she wasn't interested in working in her family's business.

As they made their way to Lincoln Center, Olivia explained her ambitious plans for the future and Sergio found himself even more smitten. She was not only beautiful, but intelligent and business minded. And he learned she had a brown "pet" cow named Betsy with a heart shaped patch of white fur on her forehead. Olivia Wilson was one of a kind.

After Sergio escorted her to Vera and Henry Delair in plenty of time to get ready, he kissed Olivia on the cheek. Her eyes widened in surprise. Her skin warm and soft, she smelled of lavender. In front of the cameras and film crew documenting the show, he stiffened in his pants and quickly excused himself before he embarrassed them all.

He took his seat in the front row, next to Allegra Vanetti and donned his dark sunglasses. Allegra was impeccably dressed in a black lace jumpsuit and satin floor length skirt suit combination.

She raised a curious brow over her own dark shades. *"Questo è interessante."*

Anxious for the Delcinia show to begin, Sergio merely shrugged. They were friends, but he didn't owe her an explanation for his attendance at the show.

Nervous energy spiked through him when Vera Delair's voice boomed through the venue's speaker system, on schedule, nearly thirty minutes late.

"Welcome everyone! Are you ready for the Delcinia Darlings?"

The crowd, made up of various celebrities, musicians, influencers, journalists, and the press, cheered and whistled their enthusiasm.

"Then let the show begin!"

The massive screen placed at the starting point of the long, wide runway displayed multi-colored fireworks exploding and much of the crowd eagerly got to their feet. He and Allegra remained seated.

The crowd counted along with the count-down...

"Ten!"

"Nine!"

"Eight!"

"Seven!"

"Six!"

"Five!"

"Four!"

"Three!"

"Two!"

"One!"

"Please welcome our first performer, the amazing Estella Cole!"

Estella emerged to thunderous applause and cheers from the crowd. The award-winning pop star, was sexily dressed in a blue sequin, sleeveless mini dress. She began belting out her current hit and proceeded about a third of the way down the runway before looking back. She paused after the first verse of her chart topper.

"And now, making her debut on a Delcinia runway, please welcome Delcinia's new lead darling, Olivia Wilson!"

The roar of the crowd was deafening as Estella resumed singing and like a dream, Olivia appeared in a purple satin and lace corset that pushed up and accentuated her luscious tits and matching tiny purple satin and lace panties. The satin and lace coordinating robe flowed on the runway floor several feet behind her, and she proceeded toward Estella with a huge smile on her face. Olivia was sexy as sin, but wholesomely beautiful at the same time.

Sergio's eyes stung, suddenly overwhelmed for Olivia. Had Henry and Vera prepared her for this? Had the other models offered guidance and encouragement rather than jealousy? Olivia was alone without her family to support her in this new and exciting phase of her life. He felt unexpectedly protective of her.

Estella reached for Olivia's hand when she reached the singer. Estella continued singing as she held Olivia's hand high and they both proceeded farther down the runway to enthusiastic applause. About halfway down, Estella elegantly let go and Olivia gracefully floated the rest of the way, flung her flowing robe behind her, singing along with the crowd and turned to complete her first runway walk.

Sergio wiped away a tear that slipped below his sunglasses. He heard Allegra grunt beside him. He ignored her.

When Olivia approached him and Allegra along the center of the runway where they were seated, she blew him a kiss and winked. The crowd went wild, and Sergio's heart nearly burst out of his chest.

Allegra snickered. *"Davvero molto interessante."*

Interesting didn't begin to cover the myriad of emotions Sergio was experiencing. Before he knew it Olivia had reached the front of the runway, offered the crowd a quick wave and disappeared.

The remainder of the show proceeded in a blur with five other female performers and over fifty other girls showcasing Delcinia's exquisite lingerie collection.

Sergio's heart nearly stopped when Olivia appeared wearing a white veil and the skimpiest but sexiest wedding lingerie set complete with white lacy and lattice G-string exposing the plump globes of her ass, dotted mesh ruffles on the matching bra, lattice and specialty trim garter belt and straps with bow clips and skinny bow accents, finished off with sheer white, lace topped thigh high stockings. She waved the small red rose bouquet as she paraded down the runway and stunned him when she tossed it to him.

"And the plot thickens," Allegra commented in English.

Sergio didn't respond, but Allegra wasn't wrong.

An hour later, following the after-show festivities, interviews, and backstage filming with the Delcinia Darlings, Sergio and Olivia rode the elevator, hand in hand up to her hotel room on the twentieth floor. After his goodbye kiss before the show, everyone assumed he and Olivia were together and neither of them corrected the impression.

Olivia turned and hugged him tightly when they reached her door. He savored the warm feel of her body against his. "Thank you for everything today. I know you were expected at the Martinez Designs show." She kissed him on the cheek and promptly blushed.

Sergio ran a finger along the smooth line of Olivia's jaw and her eyes drifted closed. "I didn't want to be anywhere else." It was the truth, regardless of how he assumed his father felt about it if all the ignored calls and texts were any indication. Sergio would deal with him later.

The chemistry between them was undeniable, but Sergio was hesitant. Olivia was only twenty to his thirty-two years. She was just beginning a new adventure, and he was an established mid-level executive at Martinez Designs. He *should* leave her alone, but she was too precious and he was too selfish to walk away.

"Stay," Olivia whispered when she opened her eyes, hunger flaring in the blue depths.

Unwilling to deny himself, Sergio captured her mouth, and they came together in a frenzied, hungry kiss that left them both panting.

Olivia quickly ushered them inside her room and in a mad rush they undressed, tossing their clothing on the floor as they made their way to the king size bed. He'd seen her nearly naked on the Delcinia runway, but her glorious naked form spread out just for him against the white bedsheets took his breath away. Perfection. And his, at least for tonight. He grabbed a condom from his pants and tossed it on the nightstand.

Sergio positioned himself on top of her, Olivia's body heat soothing his soul. He claimed her mouth again in a greedy kiss before grazing his tongue against her beaded nipple. She squirmed beneath him. He wanted to taste every inch of her delectable flesh, but his rigid cock ached to slide deeply inside of her. Sergio didn't want to rush, but he was also anxious to fuck her as soon as he could.

He nibbled and licked his way to the tiny patch of trimmed blonde hair between Olivia's legs. He inhaled her arousal and felt a burst of male pride. She wanted him as much as he wanted her.

His thumbs parted her wet folds and Olivia arched into him as he flicked his tongue against her swollen clit. Encouraged by her moans, Sergio worked her pussy until she came apart, pulsing against his tongue and gasping for air.

With shaking hands, he managed to sheath himself. Sergio would never forget the dreamy expression on Olivia's face when he thrust his aching cock inside her incredibly tight heat. She wrapped her long legs around his hips drawing him deeper inside her snug pussy. Nothing had ever felt so amazing, and Sergio had had his fair share of lovers over the years.

Olivia was wet and wild, her hunger matching his. She thrust her hips and gyrated against him as he pistoned in and out of her welcoming body. His thick shaft stretched her to her limits, and he knew he wouldn't last long. He rubbed her distended clit when he felt his spine tingle and after a few last powerful strokes, they both came, their bodies shuddering in release.

Olivia held him tight as their breathing slowed and returned to normal. As if in complete sync with each other, they both sighed in unison. Reluctantly he rolled off and lay beside her, already eager to take her again. He was certain he'd never get enough.

A satisfied smile curved her lips, and Sergio felt ten feet tall. When her stomach growled her eyes widened and a blush stained her cheeks.

"I know people in this joint. Would you like me to order us room service and we can both clean up before the food is delivered?" He'd bet she'd been too nervous to eat before the show and was most likely famished. After they were fed and energized, all bets were off.

"That would be great, thank you." Olivia gave him a quick brush of her lips and disappeared into the bathroom.

Sergio braced himself as he connected his cell phone call.

"Now you fucking answer the phone?" his father Carlos snarled.

"Dad, calm down." Sergio's gut clenched, knowing full well his father was probably fit to be tied. He was so tired of his father's attitude most of the time.

"Calm down? After you betrayed your family for some...some *underwear* model?" Carlos spat out like he was describing a prostitute. Was his father serious with this shit?

Sergio's body tensed and his jaw clenched. Olivia was a good girl from a hard-working, successful family with an exciting future ahead of her. He wouldn't allow his father to besmirch her that way.

"Jesus Christ. I didn't betray anyone. It's not my company, it's yours and Tía Silvia's. It was important that the two of *you* were there, not me."

"Your place was with us, not with some stranger," his father insisted, like Sergio was a child.

Olivia was no longer a stranger. She was so much more. Someone special to him.

"I'm a grown man, *Padre*. *I* decide my place, not you." The nerve of the man.

His father unleashed a string of curses, and Sergio hung up. He promptly turned his phone off and tossed it toward his clothes on the floor. Fuck his father's obnoxious attitude and unacceptable demands and expectations. Sergio had an amazing evening ahead of him and wasn't about to allow his father to fuck it up.

Chapter Two

March – Ten years later

Sergio rubbed his temple, standing in his father's office, his head throbbing. This was what his life had become over the last nine years since his aunt Silvia passed away from lung cancer and his mother had been taken from them three weeks later by a massive brain aneurysm. His sister Antonella, now the head designer at Martinez Designs, sat in a guest chair nearly in tears.

He'd stepped up, after his father's guilt initiative had sucked him in, and ended up spending nearly three years in Bogotá cleaning up the mess the Colombian manufacturing operation had become, and as a result, he'd also lost Olivia. The most painful loss of all. And a loss he still had not recovered from.

Sergio was done. He was no longer willing to put his personal and professional life on the back burner to carry out his father's bidding. Enough was enough.

"It's been Antonella and *me* who have propelled the company forward despite your incessant meddling. Dealing with you is a fucking nightmare, and I'm finished."

Antonella gasped, probably understanding Sergio's time at Martinez Designs was over. He hated leaving her and his younger sister Valeria behind, but Sergio needed to move on. It was past time.

"Still upset about that...girl? You're pathetic," his father snarled.

Rage burned in his gut. "Her name is Olivia, you know that. You sound like you're jealous of her. But this isn't about her, since you know she hasn't spoken to me in years because of *you*. This is about *you*. You and your brothers are *tailors*, *I'm* the one with an MBA from Wharton."

His father waved a dismissive hand, as if Sergio's Ivy League education and years of sacrifice for the family business meant nothing. Fuck that *and* Carlos Martinez.

"If you leave today, don't bother coming back."

Sergio scoffed. "Don't worry. I won't. I gave you more than you deserved for far too long. I'm finished."

Sergio left his father, hearing Antonella's raised voice as he made quick work of getting to his office down the hall. He couldn't wait to get the hell out of the building and never return. He was moments away from his freedom.

He took a speedy glance around his office and felt nothing but despair and regret. It had become his prison cell. Years ago, his desk held framed pictures of him and Olivia. Now, there was nothing personal anywhere. Sergio grabbed his briefcase and took one last look around before leaving, finally taking his life back at forty-two. What he'd do with it, he wasn't sure, but at least it was now up to *him* to decide. Not his tyrant of a father.

About thirty minutes later, Sergio found himself pacing his Uncle Brooks's office at the Grand Walhstrom. His wife, Sergio's Aunt Margot was wiping her tears with a tissue, leaning against a bookcase.

"Carlos hasn't been the same since Silvia and Justine passed," she said weakly, as if it was an acceptable excuse for his father.

Brooks nodded.

Sergio was having none of it. "He's *always* been difficult. He's gotten *worse* since they passed away. I should have left the company years ago." What a fool he'd been, staying as long as he had.

Brooks sighed, conceding with Sergio's assessment. "You've always been welcome at Walhstrom's. Just say the word, we'd love to have you join us. I know Mom and Dad would be over the moon to have you and your sisters here."

Sergio jiggled the car keys in his pants pocket while he paced. The Walhstrom side of the family had spent years trying to convince him to come work for them. His father's guilt trips had kept him at Martinez Designs. Now that he was free to do as he saw fit, he wasn't sure joining the Walhstrom family business was the best course of action.

"I don't know, but thank you again for the offer. Can I think about it?" Sergio loved the Walhstrom side of his family dearly and didn't want to hurt their feelings. He just needed a moment to get his head on straight before deciding his next move.

His Aunt Margot wrapped her comforting arms around him, and Sergio held her tight. His eyes stung as he was emotionally drained.

"Have you spoken with Olivia about any of this," Margot asked after ending their hug.

He grunted, shaking his head. "Five years ago was the last time I reached out to her and was ignored. I haven't tried again since. I'm afraid our time together is truly over." Again, because of his asshole of a father.

"That's a shame. We all adored her and had high hopes for both of you," Brooks said and got up from behind his mahogany executive desk to join Sergio and Margot.

"Why not join us for lunch downstairs at Walhstrom Italiano? We can help you strategize and calmly talk through your options. They have gnocchi in vodka sauce with Italian sausage crumbles on the menu today." Margot knew that was one of Sergio's favorites. It was a tempting and delicious offer.

When the three of them entered the restaurant a few minutes later, he noticed Henry Delair sitting alone in a large corner booth. He had two empty cocktail glasses in front of him, but no food. Where was Vera?

Sergio gestured to his aunt and uncle, and they nodded. Without asking they joined Henry in his booth. Henry glanced at them in surprise and what appeared to be relief. Something was definitely wrong.

A server appeared within moments. "Let's all have lunch and talk," Sergio said to Henry.

Henry's eyes teared up and he nodded. "Sure, thanks."

Three hours later with full stomachs, and Vera now with them, they all sat in silence, Sergio stunned and contemplating their hours' long conversation. Sergio glanced at his aunt and uncle, unsure of what to say. They offered reassuring smiles.

"Vera, are you absolutely certain you want to go through with this?" Sergio was still reeling from the news Henry had shared before Vera had joined them for lunch. She had an inoperable brain tumor with possibly only a few months left to live. Devastating news.

"Yes. It seems we're both at a crossroads, dear. Maybe it's fate's timing. All I know is I want to spend my remaining days with sand between my toes, ocean sunsets, and the sound of waves, not beeping medical machines," Vera admitted softly.

"With you at the helm and Brooks and Margot added to the board, we know the company will be in good hands. Let's move ahead, get the paperwork signed, share the news with the Darlings and issue a press release," Henry said, sounding more upbeat than when they'd first joined him.

"How do you think Olivia is going to react to the news?" Margot asked of no one in particular.

That was the million-dollar question, and if Sergio had to guess, he'd guess she'd be furious. And he couldn't blame her. Not for the first time since they'd begun discussing it, he reconsidered moving forward with the deal to purchase Delcinia.

Olivia couldn't stop smiling on her Zoom call with her sister Natalie, who was now twenty-four, and her youngest sister Faith, who was twenty-one. Olivia was now thirty. Where the hell had the time gone?

She was pleased as she reviewed the quarterly sales figures from her company Liv's Lavish Lips, her line of organic lip balm and silky, gradual plumping lip glosses. The glosses were available in several different colors. Her product line was manufactured in small batches in Orville, Ohio, on her family's farm property.

"The three new colors we introduced are selling well, Liv," Natalie announced proudly.

"It looks like we're going to need to hire people to keep up with the increased sales." Faith added happily.

Olivia was so proud of the women her sisters had grown up to be. Natalie had recently earned her MBA and Faith was pursuing a finance degree. Olivia was also proud of everything *she'd* accomplished since arriving in New York ten years before. She'd sure shown Sergio's asshole of a father, who'd treated her more like some hooker than the woman who'd loved his son to the moon and back.

She chastised herself for thinking about Sergio at all. He didn't deserve her thoughts or anything else after he'd allowed his father to run him out of the country to Bogotá for what she found out ended up being nearly three years, after his Aunt Silvia and his mother had both passed away. Sergio hadn't even fought for her. For them. Even after his many declarations of undying love. Olivia had had to mourn the loss of Silvia, Justine, and the end of her relationship with Sergio alone.

But Olivia had come out the other side stronger and more determined. She'd worked hard. Traveled the world modeling for various international designers, including Valentino, Versace, Prada, Armani, Dolce & Gabbana, and Marni, thanks to her close friend Allegra Vanetti's connections. She'd carefully considered which brands she endorsed and started her own company, Liv's Lavish Lips.

Her luxury four-bedroom penthouse condo in one of the Delair-owned buildings was paid for. She'd saved and invested a significant amount of money preparing for her investment in Delcinia when she came off the runway.

And therein lay the problem. Her plans to move into management at Delcinia were supposed to come to fruition now. But over the last couple of months when Olivia had broached the subject of transitioning off the runway with Vera and Henry, she'd been politely brushed off. Until some undefined time *later*. She didn't know why, and hadn't been offered any further explanation about the delay.

From Olivia's perspective, there wasn't much time to waste. Her ideas for expansion were necessary to implement *now*. To move the company forward, become more inclusive and attract new customers.

She and her sisters discussed ideas for additional hiring at Liv's. "Sounds like a great plan, ladies. Forward me candidate resumes, and we'll review them together." They said their goodbyes and ended their Zoom session.

Olivia's phone chimed with a text message. Huh, it was from Henry requesting the Darlings to join a Zoom call with an important company announcement in an hour. Hope bloomed. Were they going to surprise her with an announcement of her new role with the company? Then dread took the place of hope. There was much to discuss and contracts to sign before her official transition to management. The announcement had to be something else. Damn it.

Deciding enough was enough, she grabbed her purse and set out to Delcinia HQ to participate in the call in person and demand the transition conversation. If Henry and Vera had changed their minds, Olivia needed to know *now*, not later, so she could make plans. As much as she'd loved the Delairs and working as their lead Darling and model, she wanted more. She always had, and had pursued her MBA for a reason. It was time for the Delairs to put up or let her go.

She was greeted by the friendly, familiar faces at Delcinia HQ about thirty minutes later. Olivia felt confident and empowered about the conversation she planned to have with Vera and Henry. She looked forward to the future, whether it was with Delcinia or not, although she hoped she wasn't forced to leave.

As she approached Henry's office with self-assured strides, the sound of Sergio's voice struck her ears, and she went completely still, stopping dead in her tracks. A knot formed in her chest and her stomach churned. What the hell was he doing in Henry's office? She'd never admit there was a tiny part of her that was happy to see him after so many years.

Why was she self-conscious that she hadn't taken more care in her appearance before coming to HQ? She hadn't bothered changing out of her black yoga pants and Delcinia sweatshirt. She squared her shoulders and lifted her chin. Fuck Sergio. She didn't care what he thought about how she looked. Not anymore.

With renewed confidence, but bracing herself, she entered Henry's office and leaned against the door frame. Although she hadn't seen Sergio in years, Olivia's body tingled with familiar but unwelcomed awareness. Damn him for looking even more handsome than he had the day he'd broken her heart years ago. He was now forty-two with a little gray sprinkled at his temples and he'd exchanged his goatee for neatly trimmed scruff. He was so gorgeous, the stupid jerk.

No matter, she had important business to discuss when the Zoom announcement was over. Vera and Henry were seated behind his desk in front of a laptop. An empty chair was between them.

They glanced up with worried expressions on their faces. Olivia's stomach fluttered and she felt overheated. She had a strong suspicion she wasn't going to be pleased by their announcement. Damn Sergio.

"It's wonderful to see you again, Olivia." The silky-smooth timbre of Sergio's voice slid over her like a sensual caress, and her heart and stomach fluttered. Traitorous body.

"I wish I could say the same, Sergio. What the hell are you doing here?" Although being nasty to him hurt her soul, she had to protect herself.

"All that will be made clear in a moment, dear," Vera said cautiously. "Sergio please come take your seat so we can begin."

Sergio gazed at her longingly before taking his seat between Vera and Henry in front of their laptop. Shit, Olivia *knew* she wasn't going to like this. She wrung her hands, waiting for the bomb to drop.

"Hello, my darlings," Vera began. "Let me record our session so those who aren't able to join us now can watch the replay." Vera clicked her mouse and then sat back in her chair.

"We wanted to share this with all of you before we issued our press release. Sergio Martinez, former COO of Martinez Designs has acquired Delcinia. Effective immediately," Henry announced.

No! Olivia gasped, feeling faint. This couldn't be happening. It had to be a mistake.

To her horror, it wasn't, as she listened to Sergio introduce himself to everyone on the call. She paced with her hands clenched as her sister Darlings took the news in stride and Sergio spewed out garbage about his enthusiasm about Delcinia, its future and answered everyone's questions.

"Thank you for your time, ladies. Vera and I are absolutely certain Delcinia's future is bright with Sergio at the helm. We'll send everyone the link to this session recording." Henry ended the call.

"With all due respect Henry, Vera – what the fuck is this?" Olivia spat out before anyone could say anything.

They all stood, and Olivia backed up toward the door. She was so furious she shook with it.

"Calm down and let me explain," Sergio said as he approached her. Olivia immediately put her hand up, and he frowned but stopped advancing.

"I can't believe you'd betray me like this," Olivia said to Henry and Vera. "I've worked my ass off all these years for *you*, while attending night school online *and* earning my MBA. To prepare for my transition into management and a stake in the company. All the ideas and plans I shared with you, which you *claimed* you wanted to implement." Had they been lying to her about their intentions from the beginning?

"Vera and Henry shared all of it with me. Nothing's changed. I want to see all your brilliant ideas implemented as soon as possible," Sergio offered enthusiastically.

Olivia's jaw fell. Was he insane? "You've got to be kidding. I'm not going to work for *you*. Absolutely not. What would dear old Dad say?" She had a fairly good idea.

Sergio's lips thinned and his eyes narrowed. Good. She'd pissed him off. It was nothing compared to the outrage *she* felt.

"Dear, why don't you close the door and let Henry and me explain?" Vera pleaded.

Olivia had already heard enough. "I'll close the door on my way out." She glared at the three of them, fury burning in her gut. "I'm done here. I quit. Thanks for nothing." She turned with her head held high and slammed the door behind her on her way out of Henry's office.

Chapter Three

Olivia stared into the night, not paying much attention to the beautiful Manhattan city skyline. She'd come home from Delcinia HQ incensed and heartbroken. The first thing she'd done was change into a purple pair of Delcinia's prototyped Essence pajamas.

The nearly weightless, silky material had been her brainchild. Nearly as smooth and gentle as actual skin, the lightweight stretch fabric felt like wearing next to nothing at all. It was a key component in Olivia's expansion plans at Delcinia that would never see the light of day. Unless she brought the product line to market herself, under her own label. It was a huge endeavor to undertake, but worth considering now. She'd worked too long and hard to abandon the idea.

She swiped at the tears that continued to fall. On the phone with her mother a little earlier, when Vera had called a third time, her mother convinced her to answer. Olivia wished she hadn't. She'd put them on a three-way call, not trusting herself without her mother's support, only to find out her employer, mentor, and close friend was dying.

Vera had asked them not to share the news with anyone as she and Henry wanted to maintain their privacy about her health as long as they could.

They were moving to Laguna Beach in two weeks. Although not happy about it, Olivia understood Vera preferring to spend her last few precious months, at peace and tranquil at their new beach-front property. She couldn't imagine what Henry must be going through. They had been a quintessential power couple for decades.

Unwilling to argue with a dying woman, Olivia had promised Vera she would put her personal feelings aside and work with Sergio as the new Delcinia owner. There was no way in hell she was going to, however. She had accomplished much on her own, was a millionaire in her own right and had a multitude of options available to her. Fuck Sergio. She had no intention of assisting in his transition as the owner and CEO of Delcinia. He was a big boy and more than capable of running the company himself.

The knock at Olivia's door startled her. She hoped it was Vera, wanting to hug and cry with her friend in private before she moved to California to live out her last days. When she opened the door to find Sergio on the other side, she didn't hesitate and slammed the door in his face.

Her anger returned toward Vera and Henry. They had no right to tell Sergio where she lived. Olivia ignored the lightness in her chest and racing pulse, angry that he still had an effect on her.

"Please let me in."

"Fuck off. You have no right to be here." How dare he!

"I know. I only want a few minutes of your time. To talk. Then I'll leave. You have my word. *Please*."

Sergio's word meant absolutely nothing to her now. She decided to let him in and give him a piece of her mind like she *should* have done years before, then kick him the hell out. Olivia had been young and naïve to the ways of love and men at the time. Not anymore.

Olivia turned away after opening the door and walked back toward the large wall of windows in her living room, fully aware of Sergio following her. She heard him remove his coat and toss it on a chair.

"They had to sell because Vera's ill. She gave me permission to tell you she's terminal with probably only a few months left," Sergio said from right behind her. He placed a hand on her shoulder, the heat of his palm warming its way through her. She stiffened but didn't move. God, how she'd missed him. His touch. His company. His *everything*.

She nodded as new tears ran down her cheeks. "I know. I spoke with her earlier." Olivia wiped her eyes and turned around to face the only man she'd ever loved, the one who had turned his back on her so viciously nine years ago. How could he have left her so easily? Had he cared about her at all?

Sergio ran a hand along her sleeve and she shivered but backed away. He raised his hands as if in surrender. Good, he got the hint, although it tore her apart not to seek comfort in his arms after learning about Vera. It was unexpected, heartbreaking news.

"What kind of fabric is this? It's...amazing. So light, barely there."

Olivia scoffed. "It's a prototype of what I wanted to introduce as Delcinia's new Essence line of pajamas and loungewear. I told you when we met that I had plans for my future with the company. It's too late now, though." Sergio had ruined everything. Again.

"They'd told me about the fabric, but I couldn't grasp what they described. The line will become a huge success. Well done. Wait a minute. What do you mean it's too late?" Sergio's praise did something for her ego, but was he serious? How could he not understand?

She laughed in his face. "You're serious, aren't you? After what you did to me? To us on my twenty first birthday?" What arrogance. "At least you waited until everyone had left the party before you dumped me. What an idiot I was. I thought you were going to propose!"

And Olivia would have said yes without hesitation. She'd known early on Sergio had been the one for her, despite his father's obvious disdain for her and her profession. She'd been thankful she'd gotten on so well with both sides of the rest of Sergio's family. Even so, his father's attitude toward her had been stressful with unneeded tension.

"I *was* going to fucking propose! But then Silvia died and Mom shortly after. I was grief-stricken and stuck."

Olivia's head spun. He'd wanted to marry her after all? How different would their lives have been if Silvia and Justine had lived?

"The operation in Colombia was a wreck. Only a few of the single mothers had been trained well enough to create quality clothing from start to finish like Silvia intended. The management staff was pitiful. Trying to honor Silvia's intent and with the constant guilt trips Dad tossed my way,

I ended up in Bogotá for much longer than I'd planned."

"Nearly three years," Olivia stated sadly.

Sergio shoved his hands in his jeans pockets and hung his head. "I transformed the Colombian operation into a well-managed division of the company, but I'd already lost what was most dear to me. I felt imprisoned there, believe me."

Olivia shook her head. In a twisted sort of way, Sergio's father might have done them a favor after all. Marrying Sergio knowing how his father felt about her wouldn't have been easy.

"Carlos got the last laugh, didn't he? Buying Delcinia. I bet he can't wait to close down operations just to spite me." Olivia had already quit, so he wouldn't get the satisfaction of firing her at least. Condescending asshole.

Sergio made himself comfortable on the chair he'd placed his coat on. Olivia was irritated that he looked like he belonged in her place.

"No. *I* bought Delcinia. I left Martinez Designs. Weren't you listening during the Zoom call? I'm through letting my father dictate my every move and using guilt to do it. I should have left a long time ago. I was a fool to put up with his shit as long as I did." Sergio let out a weary sigh and shook his head.

Olivia felt for Sergio. She recognized his family dynamics were complicated, especially after Silvia and Justine passed. But she also suspected this falling out between father and son was most likely temporary. Before long, she predicted Carlos would have his hand in Delcinia operations.

She didn't want to believe it but had to ask. "Was I part of the deal with Vera and Henry? If I was, they had no right."

Sergio glanced at her with pain in his eyes. "No, of course not. They were nothing but complimentary about you. Your work ethic. Your ideas and contributions. Their focus had to shift once

Vera got sick. You can understand that, can't you?"

Olivia was relieved, and she understood, but it didn't change things. "I do, but I stand by my resignation. Too much has happened. I won't work for you."

Sergio stood and put his coat on. Like a fool, Olivia was disappointed. How messed up was that?

"That's unfortunate because I need you. In many ways, but certainly to implement your expansion plans. With them in place, the company has a bright future." Sergio headed toward the door to leave, pausing and turning around before opening it.

"Just think about staying. I'm not going to pressure you, but think of all we can accomplish together. Come by the office tomorrow morning at ten o'clock. We can discuss if and how we can work together, amicably, and keep the Delairs' vision alive."

The following morning, Sergio sat behind his desk, formerly Henry Delair's, at Delcinia HQ, unable to concentrate and fidgeting in his chair. His laptop clock display showed it was nearly ten thirty. He sighed dejectedly. Olivia wasn't coming. He'd been hopeful the night before as he'd noted the desire in her blue gaze even though she'd been angry and hurt.

Her no show wasn't surprising, but he'd expected she would want to at least explore implementing her expansion plans. The new Essence line could be a potential game changer that included coordinating men's garments. The product line expansion into larger sizes, which was long overdue as well as the girls' college scholarship program. Sergio was on board with everything Henry and Vera had shared with him. Olivia's plans had impressed the shit out of him.

The decision to acquire Delcinia hadn't been all that difficult. There was so much potential that he couldn't turn Delair's offer down. Having his Uncle Brooks and Aunt Margot join the small board of directors was an added bonus. They had wanted to work with him for years, and now they would, on *his* terms. For *his* company.

Regardless of Olivia's decision to stay on or not, Sergio needed to address the Camille Winters "situation" right away. Vera's closest friend and with Delcinia from the very beginning as head designer and design department manager, she'd become an impediment to the company's growth initiatives.

To Sergio's astonishment and delight, although thirty minutes late, Olivia strolled into his office without knocking. Regardless of her decision about Delcinia, his heart raced and his cock twitched, he was so happy to see her again.

She still took his breath away. Flawless makeup, not that she needed any. And dressed in a curve-hugging but professional blue sweater dress that matched the shade of her sparkling blue eyes. Perfection, all these years later.

Olivia held her head high, not mentioning that she was late. "So, tell me how I might fit into *your* organization, should I decide to stay."

Hope bloomed and lust surged through his veins. Sergio gestured to the guest chairs in front of his desk. She sat down with poise; her baby blues laser focused on him. He prayed he didn't fuck up his proposal and that he could convince Olivia to stay on.

"*Our* organization. You'll have a twenty percent stake in the company." Olivia's eyes widened and Sergio was confident he had her sincere attention. When she frowned, he began doubting himself.

"The buy-in Vera, Henry, and I agreed to would have given me a five to seven percent stake. I don't have nearly enough saved for twenty." Olivia maintained her self-assured posture, but the disappointment was evident on her face.

The Delairs weren't giving Olivia enough credit. He supposed as the founders of the company, he could understand. It didn't change his perspective on the matter, however.

"Don't sell yourself short. You've been an exceptional ambassador for Delcinia. Your ideas and plans are key to the company's growth. Recruiting the Bellucci sisters as designers was a stroke of genius, propelling our international exposure."

Olivia beamed at him, and his heart swelled. The young Italian designer sister duo were hot commodities and the cousins of Italian supermodel and actress Maria Bellucci. Isabella and Sienna Bellucci were the ungettable gets, and yet Olivia had gotten them.

"Don't worry about your buy in. I'm not taking your money. I don't need it." Hell, Sergio should offer *her* a huge sign-on bonus for her stake in the company. Olivia was that critical to the company's future.

Olivia shook her head emphatically. "Absolutely not. I've been saving for this opportunity for the last ten years. You can't just give me twenty percent. I won't accept it. I want skin in the game. A vested interest, even if it's less than twenty percent."

From Sergio's perspective she had plenty of skin in the game. He admired her integrity, work ethic and business instincts. She'd come a long way from the young girl he'd met ten years ago. He was so fucking proud of her and wanted her to feel comfortable taking on this new role.

"Vera and Henry only set aside a small amount to kick off the girls' scholarship fund. Why not add your vested interest there, as we'll have a substantial kick off right out of the gate? Do more good. Help more girls." Sergio had gotten the impression the Delairs hadn't been fully on board with the scholarship program. With Olivia's investment, the effort would be meaningful, not half-assed.

Olivia laid a hand on her heart and her eyes softened with an inner glow. "I love that idea. Thank you."

Sergio's spirits soared. She appeared to be on board. "Make no mistake. You'll be my right-hand man – woman. I'll count on you heavily. I want to implement the bulk of your ideas by September's fashion week. There's a lot to do and we'll be working closely together. Long hours. I hope your boyfriend isn't the jealous type." Sergio smirked. He was aware she wasn't dating anyone. Not that it mattered to him if she did. If she agreed to stay on at Delcinia, he'd do whatever it took to win her back for good. It was *his* time now.

When she rolled her eyes, he chuckled. God, she was adorable. Still.

"That won't be an issue. I'm a professional. I'm sure Vera and Henry attested to that." Olivia stated proudly.

"Indeed, they did. And I've followed your career over the years, so I know. Do we have an agreement? Should I have your contract drafted for your attorneys to review?"

When her face turned serious, his stomach clenched. Damn it. Had he already fucked up?

"Yes. As long as you understand I intend to keep things between us strictly professional," Olivia stated with a tinge of sadness in her voice.

Sergio raised a brow. "Would it be so terrible if things between us became *un*professional?" He understood she was hurt and angry, but it didn't change the fact that the chemistry between them was scorching hot. There was still something between them. Olivia needed to let her guard down and allow things to develop, or re-develop naturally.

She glared at him, and he regretted moving too fast. Sergio couldn't help himself though. Having her this close, but still so far away, was torture.

"For me it would. I can't go through another heartbreak over you. If you can't respect that, then the best thing would be for me to leave." Olivia glanced at him expectantly but with a sadness in her eyes that broke *his* heart. He'd make it up to her, slowly earning back her trust. She was worth the wait. She was worth everything.

"I respect your wishes. Not happy about them, I admit." Sergio stood, and Olivia appeared confused. "First order of business for us is to have a conversation with Camille."

Olivia cringed. Sergio felt her pain. Camille was a legend in the business, especially with her bridal designs. But over the last few years, her designs had become a bit dated. She was resistant to the new ideas Olivia and Vera had proposed and was not pleased with the Bellucci sisters. If they couldn't bring Camille around, they'd have no choice but to let her go.

As he and Olivia entered Camille's office, she scowled. "Well, that didn't take long. Should I start packing my things?"

Sergio sighed, and his shoulders sagged. *Come on Camille, get with the program.*

"We don't want to fire you, *but* in order to move the company forward and expand we need you to be open to new ideas. Let's work together. Be a mentor to Isabella and Sienna. They're thrilled to work with you if you'd just give them an honest chance."

Camille remained silent, seemingly thinking things over. Sergio didn't want to lose her, but if he had to let her go, he would.

"Let's honor all the hard work you, Vera, and Henry have done building this company. Together we can make them proud and grow their legacy. What do you say?" Olivia pleaded.

Camille swiped a tear from her cheek. "I know you're right. I've been stubborn in my thinking. The Italians' designs are inspired. I'd be honored to work with them. Thank you for not giving up on me. I promise you won't regret it."

Olivia hugged Camille and all the tension in the room eased. "Never. You helped put this place on the map."

Camille smiled at them graciously. "I suppose I did, didn't I? I know we have a lot to do. I'd like to see about bringing your sisters on if they're open to the idea, for the larger size line."

Sergio loved that idea. Olivia's sisters would make wonderful additions to the Delcinia family.

Olivia's smile lit up the room. "I'll discuss it with them. I think they'll be excited."

"Can I say it does my heart a world of good to see you two back together again?" Camille asked with a gleam in her eyes.

Heaviness weighed on Sergio's chest when Olivia immediately shook her head.

"We're not together personally, only professionally. That ship sailed years ago." Olivia declared with a certainty that hurt Sergio to his core.

Camille shot Sergio a knowing glance, not seeming convinced. He had his work cut out for him, but a future with Olivia by his side was well worth it.

Chapter Four

A few weeks later, Olivia and Sergio slowly toured Camille's expansive office space. It was filled with mannequins showcasing various new pieces in Delcinia's Eden bridal line.

A relaxed smile crossed her lips as she gazed at the exquisite samples on display. Olivia loved everything she saw, from the corsets, silk and lace slip dresses, teddies and bustiers, to the lace panty and garter belt sets, camisoles and satin and lace elegant short robes and long robes featuring lace edged sweep trains.

Olivia nodded in delight. The designs were fresh and modern. More than she'd dared to hope for. She observed Sergio examining each piece. Carefully scrutinizing every detail. When he reached out and gently ran his fingers over a pair of lace garters, Olivia was immediately reminded of the many times he had caressed her skin. A jolt of longing shot through her, and she shuddered with lust. Not good.

As if sensing her desire, Sergio turned, a devilish smirk curving his lips. "Perfection." He whispered.

Olivia's pulse spiked as sparks blazed inside her. How many times had he whispered that very word while caressing her skin during their year together? Her body shivered recalling their intimate time together. Olivia's thoughts were fully absorbed in the memories when she was startled back to the present.

"I'm so pleased!" Camille smiled proudly.

Olivia fought hard to refocus while Sergio set a sensual stare on her. "Sergio's right. Everything *is* perfect. I'm intrigued with the robe train."

Camille nodded enthusiastically. "Yes, my thinking was to extend the wedding day into the wedding night. I'd like us to offer sweep, court, and chapel length lace edged train robe options."

Olivia loved that idea. "Maybe pair the robes with some of the racier lingerie sets for a sexy wedding night reveal. Let's try that for some of our test shots later."

A ray of need shone in Sergio's eyes, and Olivia quickly turned her attention back to Camille.

"I can't take *all* the credit. The Italians may have offered some wonderful design insights and suggestions," Camille admitted with a bright smile. "I was unsure at first, but I've enjoyed collaborating with Isabella and Sienna. Even learned a thing or two. I hope they've found our time working together beneficial too."

Olivia was relieved to hear that. She hadn't relished the idea of having to let Camille go, but would have if left with no other choice. The Italian sisters were key for their expansion plans.

Sergio nodded. "I'm glad to hear that, Camille. The feedback we've received about them has been positive. Without betraying any confidences, I can tell you they've enjoyed working with you as well. They have an enormous amount of respect for you and everything you've accomplished at the company."

Camille beamed with pride as she should. She'd been crucial in Delcinia's success to this point. Camille set up her laptop and the three of them reviewed other proposed designs for the Enchantment line, their main line consisting of bras, panties, corsets, teddies, camisoles, and more. All garments would now include even larger sizes because *every* woman should have the opportunity to feel beautiful in Delcinia lingerie, regardless of their size.

This expansion of the product line meant everything to Olivia. Her beautiful sisters had sexy curves that would look amazing in Delcinia's designs.

The exciting new Essence line, the nearly naked, barely there feeling fabric for pajamas and loungewear included coordinating men's garments. Which also meant they'd recruited some of the best-known male models in the business. Now Delcinia had male Darlings. Olivia was nearly giddy with anticipation. Her dreams and plans were finally coming to fruition.

"When we were together, I'd wanted some kind of garments to coordinate with your lingerie. I pictured us relaxing on a Sunday morning over breakfast, in matching loungewear. The Essence line captures what I had in mind back then," Sergio said wistfully while they looked over the pajamas, chemises, nightgowns, robes, and boxer styled pants.

Olivia's heart swelled. He'd wanted to match with her? He'd never mentioned it. It was an incredibly sweet idea, although it didn't matter now. It could, she reminded herself. She promptly pushed that thought away. She wasn't going to risk her heart a second time, but hoped other men felt the same about the line.

"There was one thing we were considering. Delcinia is known for our intricate lace, and this line doesn't feature any. What if we add some on the women's garments?" Camille studied the photos on her laptop, deep in thought.

Sergio remained silent, presumably awaiting Olivia's response. "Won't that weigh down the fabric, affecting the nearly naked feel? Defeating the purpose of the line entirely?" Olivia agreed Delcinia's lacework was extraordinary, but she was uncertain about adding it to the Essence line.

Sergio and Camille seemed to contemplate Olivia's concerns.

"What if we add small lace accents on the women's V-neck pajama tops, and lace straps on the chemises and cami tops?" Sergio suggested.

That wasn't a bad idea, Olivia thought. "Can we prototype and decide from there?"

Camille made some notes while she nodded. "Good idea. If those lace additions don't affect the light, sheer feel of the fabric we can offer the lace accented options."

Feeling satisfied with their decisions, the topic of discussion turned to Vera and Henry. Camille had visited Vera and Henry in Laguna Beach recently. They'd settled in and were enjoying their ocean front home. Vera was doing fairly well, considering. She'd had moments of confusion during Camille's visit that had passed somewhat quickly. Those bouts would become more frequent as her condition continued to deteriorate.

They'd arranged for in-home hospice and their competent medical team was providing Henry with the emotional support he needed. Personal visits were now limited to close family members and Camille only.

Olivia was wiping her tears when she received a text stating everyone, including her sisters, was ready to take test shots in their in-house studio.

"Have either of you said anything about September being my last show and passing the Lead Darling title to Akira?"

"Are you sure about this?" Sergio's concerned expression did something to Olivia's heart that she needed to ignore. He still wasn't on speaking terms with his father, but she knew that wouldn't last. Carlos would come around at some point, and she refused to allow him to mistreat her again in any way. Once had been enough to last her a lifetime.

"I'm sure. This was always my plan. I have commitments with some other designers I'll fulfill but after that…" Olivia wanted to concentrate on Delcinia and her lip care business.

Camille frowned, seemingly disappointed. "Don't be hasty, dear. Why not transition to an Honorary Darling? Participate in shows at your discretion when time allows and be featured in the catalog?"

"You don't have to decide right now. Take some time and think about it. Right now, everyone's waiting on us." Sergio stood, and she and Camille followed him to the studio. It made sense to her to wait before making a final decision. Camille's Honorary Darling idea had merit ands was worth serious consideration.

As Olivia changed into her first lace bra and panty set, in deep purple, her signature color, she felt pleased at the diversity the female and male Darlings now represented. From Hispanics and Blacks to Asians and Caucasians, the wonderful models showcasing Delcinia's designs reflected the diverse customer base they wanted to attract. And with her sisters as the initial larger sized models, every woman could see themselves in Delcinia's lingerie.

When Olivia emerged onto the expansive studio that included various bedroom sets, couches and other furniture, she spotted Allegra with a reassuring arm around her youngest sister Faith who was clutching her lavender silk robe tightly around her. Faith seemed on the verge of tears. Not good.

Olivia had initially been concerned when Faith had agreed to this assignment. She'd always been shy but wanted to join her sisters, Olivia and Natalie.

It didn't go unnoticed that Martina, Akira, and Fatima were all fawning over Sergio, encouraging him to get into a pair of Essence boxer pants and join them for the photo shoot. She ignored the unexpected raging jealousy and possessiveness gnawing at her insides and rushed to her sister's side.

Allegra graciously stepped back, nodding at Olivia.

"I'm sorry, Liv. I don't think I can do this. I feel so fat and ugly compared to everyone else," Faith whispered.

Faith's admission broke Olivia's heart, and she was grateful everyone else provided them some much needed space, while offering their silent support from the sidelines. Olivia would never force Faith to do something she felt uncomfortable about.

"Hey now, Faith. That's not true. You have a beautiful heart and soul. And it shines through on the outside." Olivia knew Faith to be a math and science nerd, never caring much about her appearance, but she and Natalie were knockouts.

"I've always been envious of your and Natalie's curvy hips and full tushies. Very sexy, honey. You have nothing to be embarrassed about. And you and Natalie will show all the other women who aren't a size zero that they can feel beautiful in our products."

"Because we're *all* beautiful in our own way, and we shouldn't feel self-conscious about wanting to wear luxury lingerie. We deserve to!" Natalie added.

"And trust me, *bella*, it's *confidence* that makes a woman sexy, not the number on the scale." Allegra turned to the men, quietly observing Faith's mini-meltdown. "Am I right, *ragazzi*?"

The men all murmured their agreement and nodded, smiling at Faith.

Allegra's words seemed to have a positive effect on Faith as she stood tall and proud, nodding decisively. Her eyes were bright, and her smile was sweet, like the girl herself.

"What do you say we show the world how amazing the Wilson sisters are?" Olivia couldn't wait to introduce her sisters to their customer base around the globe.

"Yes. Let's do this!"

"*Mierda.*" Sergio wiped up the marble kitchen counter where he'd spilled black sauce. He'd invited Olivia over for dinner after the shoot so they could review the girls' scholarship program.

Once Faith had calmed down, and they'd gotten through a few test shots with the Wilson sisters in different shades of purple, smirking at the camera, giving it the finger, the session including the male Darlings had gone well. He was confident they would expand their customer base.

His favorite photo of the day had been of the Wilson sisters posing with a curved white overstuffed chaise lounge. Olivia lay on the lounge, with Natalie standing beside her and Olivia's arm wrapped around Natalie's thigh. Faith sat on the ground in front of Olivia with an arm draped over Olivia's legs. It was a stunning photo and a wonderful introduction of the sister trio.

The male and female models coalesced perfectly in various shots. Some sensual with the Enchantment lingerie pieces and others more "family friendly" with the new Essence line. Good natured flirting between the men and women wouldn't have bothered him if it hadn't included Olivia. The men didn't realize Olivia was off limits.

When she'd been paired up with Nigerian Chiemeka, or Cooper as he was called, for some test shots with the Eden line, Sergio had nearly lost his shit. When she'd appeared wearing the chapel length bridal robe with a lacy garter belt set underneath, he'd been close to demanding to take Cooper's place as Fatima and Akira had suggested unabashedly while flirting with him.

It could have been his imagination, but it had seemed that Olivia had been jealous of the women's overtures toward him. There was nothing to be jealous of. Regardless, Sergio was no model, but watching Cooper with Olivia in a bridal scenario had pissed him the fuck off.

How many times had he imagined his and Olivia's wedding night? A million, that was how many. And watching it play out, albeit fake, in front of the camera with another man, had made Sergio's blood boil. *They* were supposed to be together, damn it.

Working so closely together the past few weeks and not being able to take Olivia in his arms and love her like he'd wanted to do for so long, had been bittersweet torture. She'd warmed up to him over the past weeks but had kept her interactions with Sergio annoyingly professional.

At least she hadn't pulled away when he'd placed a hand on her shoulder or extended kind physical and non-physical gestures not meant to be sexual. He'd promised himself he wouldn't push her, but he was anxious to pursue a personal relationship with her. To make up for all the lost years his father had snatched from them. There wasn't a moment to waste.

The doorbell rang just as he'd finished setting the table. The *posta cartagenera* (black sauce pork) with the sauce on the side as Olivia preferred, rice and salad were ready to serve.

Sheer joy overtook him when Sergio opened the door of his townhome mansion, previously owned by the late fashion legend Dario Balestra. He found Olivia makeup free, holding her laptop bag ready to work, but her inner light shined brightly.

Olivia inhaled deeply and moaned. Sergio's cock stirred. "Is that *posta cartagenera*?"

He knew it was one of her favorite Colombian dishes. He was no dummy. He was intent to impress. "It is. Are you hungry?"

Olivia's smile seemed strained and didn't reach her eyes, but she nodded. "Lead the way. We've got a lot of work to do."

Sergio nearly growled, leading her to the small dining area facing the expansive first floor courtyard. She sat down and immediately powered up her laptop. Rather than argue, he buried his disappointment and brought their dinner to the table. His mouth watered at the sight of Olivia at the table wearing an off-the-shoulder purple sweater. He ached to get his hands and mouth on her delectable flesh.

They ate in companionable silence for a moment. Sergio didn't want to work. He wanted to show Olivia the fourteen thousand square foot home he'd purchased with their future in mind. He'd spent considerable time and money renovating the six floors and rooftop terrace with gazebo to accommodate the future family he desperately wanted with her.

Olivia handed Sergio a stack of scholarship applications, and Sergio reluctantly accepted them. So much for a possible romantic evening, he mused unhappily. But the program was important, so he concentrated on the task at hand while they finished dinner. At least Olivia seemed to enjoy what he'd prepared for her. A small miracle, but he'd take it.

"We have a wonderful group of candidates. This program is going to change lives," Olivia said with much less enthusiasm than he'd expected. It was surprising, considering the scholarship program was her passion project, and he was fully on board.

Sergio pressed on, now wanting to get the evening over with so he could be alone and lick his emotional wounds.

"On the website, let's offer weekly sale items on a new scholarship fund page that contributes to the fund. We can add a direct donation link," he suggested.

Olivia nodded, seemingly distracted. What the hell?

Undeterred, Sergio continued. "We need larger and corporate doners to make the program an on-going success. We should plan a yearly fundraising charity black tie event with the Darlings in attendance and scholarship winners who will share their stories. Best to host it after February or September Fashion Week."

"Uh huh," Olivia muttered.

Sergio gritted his teeth, struggling to control his temper. "What? What's wrong with my ideas? What's bothering you?" Frustration bubbled. They were essentially finished with their business so Olivia could leave if that was what she wanted.

"I could ask you the same. What's wrong with *you*?" Olivia snapped back.

Sergio bolted out of his chair, so annoyed he couldn't stand it. He nearly kicked the overstuffed couch adjacent to the windows facing the courtyard. He shoved his hands in his pants pockets and turned around. Olivia glared back at him.

"Fine, you want to know what's wrong with me? I'm pissed. And jealous, okay? You don't even seem to want to be here, and it was your idea to get moving on the scholarship program. Are you anxious to get back to Chiemeka and his harem?" Sergio was such a dope, as he didn't want to know where Olivia would rather be other than with him.

Olivia gasped and stood, her eyes darkening. "What are you talking about? Cooper's gay, you idiot, so no I'm not rushing back to his *male* harem. And even if he wasn't and I wanted to rush back, what business is it of yours? Why do you care?"

Cooper's sexuality was a small consolation. Olivia approached him, but Sergio stood his ground. "You know why."

"What about you? I thought we'd have to wait on your threesome with Fatima and Akira before we started the shoot. Why not include Faith in your little escapade? She's always had a crush on you."

Sergio knew that but had always considered Faith's crush sweet. Harmless. His lips twitched with satisfaction knowing Olivia had been jealous of *him*. It was a start. Maybe all wasn't lost after all.

"Don't be ridiculous. I wasn't flirting with them. They were flirting with *me*. And you're one to talk. You did your fair share with Liam and Julian, in addition to Cooper. I noticed, you know?" That might have been her plan all along. To fuck with him.

Olivia had the nerve to scoff at him. "That flirting or schmoozing never meant anything to me. Sort of goes with the territory. It never bothered you before. Why now?"

Was she serious? "Because, damnit. Back then you loved me. Back then you were mine."

Olivia's eyes widened and her pupils dilated. The denied passion of years spent apart simmered between them. They belonged together, and Sergio was determined to convince her of that, one way or another.

They came together with raw need, their lips claiming each other's. Olivia trembled in Sergio's arms while he poured everything he had into his ravenous kisses. They ended their kisses breathing hard.

Sergio hurried them to the couch but not before removing Olivia's purple sweater, exposing her pretty lace purple bra and beautiful flesh. God, how he'd missed her. They made quick work of undressing, Sergio grabbing a condom from his wallet before tossing his pants aside.

He gently laid Olivia down on the soft couch like the precious treasure she was to him. He carefully took his place on top of her, Olivia's soft warmth giving him the comfort he'd craved for far too long. Their closeness was like a drug, lulling Sergio into ecstasy.

Sergio claimed Olivia's lips, raining hungry, desperate kisses on her. He kissed her again and again, losing count, the world melting away.

He nipped at her ear and smiled when she shivered in response. Sergio then trailed his lips along her collarbone to the hollow of her throat, kissing her racing pulse, the taste of her warm skin divine.

His mouth wandered to her breasts, capturing the tight bud of her nipple and sucking until she groaned her pleasure, writhing beneath him. Sergio nearly came right then when Olivia tugged on his hair, making his scalp sting.

Sergio reveled in the joy of rediscovering his one and only love when he teased the swollen nub of her clit. His tongue lashed at her drenched pussy, driving Olivia wild until with a final yank of his hair, she came apart, pulsing against his tongue.

He tore at the condom wrapper, unable to wait to finally have her again. Pride surged through him, seeing Olivia limp and satisfied, her gleaming blue eyes dreamy. He was grateful and relieved he could still please her.

When she reached out to him, he didn't hesitate, parted her thighs and pushed himself into her tight heat with one firm thrust. Her pussy stretched to accommodate his hard cock, pulsating around him. Olivia locked her legs around him, making Sergio her willing captive.

Hearts racing, bodies reunited, they moved together as one after so many years apart. His thick stalk hammered into her over and over again, Olivia's hips meeting his thrusts, stroke for stroke. She grabbed his ass pulling him deeper inside her snug cunt, Sergio grunting out his delirious pleasure. This was home, where he belonged. It had been since the day they'd met and it always would be.

"I've missed you so much *cariña*," he whispered, on the verge of coming.

"I've missed you too, but–"

Sergio claimed her lips, refusing to tarnish their long-fought moment with a discussion about the past. There would be plenty of time for that later.

Her pussy gripped him as he pistoned in and out of her with hard, sure, possessive strokes. They came in an intense shared release, blazing hot like the sun.

They lay together languidly as night had fallen, Sergio's head nestled between her breasts. Eyes closed and his breathing slowly returning to normal, with Olivia's arms wrapped around him, he'd never felt more at peace. He never wanted to move.

"I've never stopped loving you. I can't pretend I don't want us together again," Sergio whispered into the night. He felt Olivia stiffen beneath him, but she didn't let go of him.

"I'm not sure it's a smart idea to rekindle our relationship. So much time has passed. Your father hates me. That hasn't changed. I can't risk another heartbreak because of him." Olivia sounded so crestfallen; tears welled in her eyes.

Sergio understood her concerns, but everything was different now. "I promise you, I don't care what my father thinks. I never really did. We're not even on speaking terms. I'm my own man and exactly where I want to be."

Olivia didn't say a word but clutched him tight. Sergio was grateful and let the relief sink in. He wouldn't rush her. He believed in time she'd feel confident in them. In their future together.

Chapter Five

July

Olivia playfully kicked at the warm ankle-deep water in Santa Rosa Beach while Sophisto Moda Magazine's photographer snapped his shots and the film crew captured every moment. Although it was nearly ninety degrees in the hot Florida sun, she felt exhilarated.

She'd chosen a skimpy deep plum colored bikini with a Brazilian bottom and ample butt cheek peek and accented with matching plum colored beaded fringe around the waist and along the leg openings. The underwire bikini top also had beaded fringe along the straps for added sparkle and movement. Olivia frolicked in the shallow water not paying much attention to the photographer.

Olivia still couldn't believe she'd been chosen as one of the Thirty, Flirty, and Fabulous women in their thirties for the special edition of the magazine. She was humbled to be among the exceptional performers, celebrities, business owners, and politicians being featured in the issue, and was assured her close friendship with Allegra Vanetti hadn't played a part in her selection.

Her shoot in Santa Rosa Beach with its pristine beauty, turquoise waters and glorious, white-sand shores couldn't have come at a better time. Olivia had been burning the midnight oil between Liv's Lavish Lips and preparing for Fashion Week in September, and the scholarship charity fundraising ball, the week after.

When Allegra had suggested they take three days and discover local boutiques, browse art galleries and indulge in award-winning cuisine, Olivia had immediately agreed, although she missed Sergio terribly.

She and Allegra had enjoyed a laid-back getaway short on crowds but long on relaxation. Santa Rosa Beach was an idyllic combination of upscale amenities and stretches of sand where you never struggled to find a place to spread out your beach towel. They were staying at the award-winning Walhstrom Coral Waters Resort, literally several yards from the photo shoot itself.

"I've got everything I need, hun," the photographer called out.

"Great, thanks!" Olivia closed her eyes and tilted her head up to the sun with a smile on her face. She heard the click of the camera but didn't care. She trusted Allegra's staff to select the most flattering shots for her piece.

Allegra's assistant waited with a white linen oversized shirt cover up when Olivia walked back to shore. About to join Allegra, already relaxing on a white lounge chair under a huge blue umbrella, Olivia spotted Sergio in khaki cargo shorts and a white polo shirt making his way down the white wooden stairs leading from the hotel to the beach.

She squealed in delight and raced to meet him. Happiness filled her. Sergio caught her deftly when she leaped into his arms. He twirled her around in the sand as they both laughed with glee.

"What an amazing surprise." Olivia brushed her lips against his, mindful of everyone around them and the film crew.

Sergio clasped her hand and escorted her to the empty lounge chair beside Allegra, who lifted her piña colada in salute. "Are you joining Olivia for her interview?"

He helped Olivia settle into her lounge chair and she took a refreshing, fruity sip of her strawberry daiquiri.

"This is Olivia's time to shine. I'm here for *after* the interview."

Olivia's body heated, and her stomach tingled anticipating what would most likely happen after the interview. Could the day be any more perfect?

Sergio excused himself and got comfortable in a lounge chair far enough away from Olivia and Allegra to ensure their privacy. She heard him ask Allegra's assistant for a Corona.

Allegra clicked on her small digital voice recorder. "International super model. MBA. Business mogul. These are some of the words that describe the illustrious Olivia Wilson. Please tell our readers how you've accomplished so much at only thirty."

Olivia blushed at Allegra's praise. She was one to talk. Although older than Olivia at fifty-five, Allegra had accomplished just as much for her family's mass media empire. Even more.

"I think it really began with the support and encouragement of my parents. My father met my mother when they were young. She was a veterinary tech at the time and to my father, she seemed to know as much about animals as the veterinarian she worked for. He encouraged her to think big, take a chance on herself, and enroll in veterinary school."

"How forward thinking of him, wouldn't you say?" Allegra asked.

Olivia nodded. It had been. "I agree. They were married long before she graduated, but she's the main vet at my family's dairy farm and has four offices in and around Orville, Ohio. She employs many women, and she and my father have encouraged me and my sisters to pursue our dreams, even if they didn't include working for Wilson Dairy." Olivia loved them all the more for their unconditional support.

She and Allegra continued the interview as if they were just having a friendly conversation. Topics ranged from what it took to be successful, especially for a woman, to hobbies and how Olivia spent her down time. Since Sergio had joined them, she'd expected Allegra to ask about her love life.

"If I recall, in your early days with Delcinia, you and Sergio Martinez were quite the *It Couple* for about a year. And now you're back together and partners at Delcinia." Because Vera was dying. Olivia was grateful Allegra hadn't brought that up. It was too painful to talk about and wasn't common knowledge.

"Yes, that's true. We came together when I was just starting out and very young. And we spent quite a few years apart." She chose her words carefully and wasn't about to bring up Sergio's father as the reason for their breakup. "Reuniting personally and professionally after so much time apart was unexpected, but so far it's been wonderful."

The threat of Carlos Martinez destroying their relationship a second time always loomed in the back of Olivia's mind, but she was enjoying her and Sergio's "love bubble" too much to walk away. She was older now and was confident she could handle the fallout should the worst come to pass. Her position with Delcinia was iron clad as stated in her contract, so she had no worries there.

After the interview ended, she and Sergio joined Allegra for a quick bite to eat on Allegra's hotel suite's balcony with a lovely coastal view. Conversation and laughs flowed freely while they enjoyed tropical chicken, shrimp scampi skewers, and bone-in beef short ribs with rice pilaf and green beans as sides. They'd left Allegra's when she'd received a business call from Milan she needed to take.

She and Sergio immediately began shedding their clothes the moment they'd closed and locked Olivia's suite door. The spacious rotunda suite offered panoramic views of the beach, as well as brilliant sunrises and magnificent sunsets from the balcony. Valuing her privacy, Olivia had pulled down and secured the shades before she'd left the room for the day's activities.

Sergio led her to the balcony by the hand after they'd undressed, not that there was much to remove. He sprawled out on the thickly cushioned lounge chair, quickly sheathed his rigid cock, and guided Olivia down to straddle his lap.

Olivia's mouth covered his, her calm shattered with the hunger of their kisses. Sergio's lips were warm and firm as he gave of himself freely. His voracious kisses sent the pit of her stomach into a wild swirl, and her core slickened.

She rubbed her damp pussy along his thick stalk, the friction against her sensitive clit causing intense pleasure to swamp her senses. The rush of heat consumed her, and a greedy orgasm tore through her. Olivia slumped over Sergio, trying to catch her breath.

He held her for a moment, his skin warm and damp. "Ride me, *mi amor*. Fuck me hard," Sergio whispered, his voice deep, rough, and commanding.

Bolstered by her own frenzied desire, Olivia quickly lowered herself, guiding his thick length inside her, her body adjusting to accommodate his size.

Sergio gripped her hips, and Olivia met the driving rhythm he set for them. He lifted her up and down on his throbbing cock at a near frantic pace. She threw her head back and moaned her pleasure, her breasts bouncing from the force of their fucking.

When his movements became jerky, he slipped his hand between her legs and rubbed her engorged clit with deft fingers, sending her over the edge with soul-wrenching satisfaction. He followed her over shortly after with a low groan, pulsing his release inside her.

Their sweaty foreheads touched, and neither said a word. They listened to the calming sounds of the crashing waves wrapped in bliss.

"I love you so much, but I'm terrified something is going to happen to tear us apart again," Olivia whispered into the night, her eyes still closed. She'd meant Sergio's father. He was Carlos's only son. They'd eventually make amends. Where would that leave her? Them?

Sergio caressed her back, sending a shiver down her spine. "Nothing's going to happen. You're my heart and soul. *El amor de mi vida*. Always."

Olivia wanted to believe but was unsure. "He's your father. You're his only son." Not that Sergio needed a reminder.

He kissed her bare shoulder and fireworks tingled through her body. "He was my tormentor. My warden. You have no idea the sheer joy I felt when I quit Martinez Designs and reclaimed my life. There is nothing he could say or do, *ever*, that would cause me to walk away. My life, my way." Sergio seemed so certain.

Olivia was torn. He sounded sincere and she knew from what Sergio and his sisters had shared with her that Carlos was "difficult," even before Justine and Silvia had passed away.

"Let me prove myself to you. Move in with me. You already have a few of your things at my place. Move the rest in. Keep your condo for security. Let's take our shot and grab the happiness we were so unfairly robbed of."

Oh my God. She bit her lower lip, willing herself to believe they truly had a future together this time around. Sergio seemed earnest now, she prayed his mindset didn't change when he and his father eventually reconciled.

Still though, Olivia needed to be cautious. It was the prudent thing to do. She had to protect herself. "Can I think about it?"

Sergio chuckled beneath her, and their bodies jiggled. "Of course. I'm thrilled you're willing to consider it."

Sergio took one last glance around the former dressing room with adjoining bathroom that he'd converted into a spacious office for Olivia. It was directly across the hall from his office / library on the third level of his, now their home. It had been three short weeks since their time in Santa Rosa Beach, and surprisingly Olivia had agreed to move in with him. Moving day had finally arrived.

He'd been smiling so much since he'd woken up his jaw ached, but he didn't care. Sergio's first and only love was going to share in his life completely.

Both professionally and now personally. Sergio was a lucky man. And so, so grateful.

Olivia had decided, with his encouragement, to keep her condo. She'd had the movers bring her clothing, mementoes, office furniture, various accent pieces and some kitchen appliances including an ice cream maker. He couldn't wait. Wilson Dairy's super premium ice cream was the absolute best, and he had a Wilson living with him now to make it just for him. Lucky as fuck was more like it.

Sergio's sister Antonella, the lead designer at Martinez Designs, and her partner Elisa, a marketing executive at the company had eagerly volunteered to help out on moving day. His youngest sister Valeria was on a date with her new boyfriend and couldn't join them.

He worried about his youngest sister. She was only twenty-five and had always been shy with the opposite sex. A numbers nerd with a big heart who unfortunately still lived with his father. Sergio had offered to let her move in with him after he'd left Martinez Designs, but she'd declined, assuring him she'd be fine and wanted to find her own place soon anyway.

Sergio didn't particularly care for Valeria's new boyfriend either. Diego Alvarez, youngest son of Fernando Alvarez, otherwise known as the "condo king of Florida," was cocky and entitled. *Not* who Sergio would have chosen for his baby sister. He'd keep an eye on the arrogant thirty-year old Alvarez and step in if he saw fit, whether Valeria liked it or not.

Anxious to see Olivia moving around *their* home, he rushed up the stairs forgoing the elevator to the fourth floor, housing their full-floor master suite, with an enormous dressing room and a double bathroom spa. He was looking forward to spending their first night together as live-ins after Antonella and Elisa left.

"*Querida*," Sergio called out when he entered what would be their sanctuary from now on.

"In the closet."

Sergio's body flashed and sizzled in an all-consuming heat. The closet had a comfy, overstuffed couch. They had some time before he needed to fire up the grill in the courtyard and feed everyone. Perfect timing.

He was surprised to find Olivia seated on the couch wearing white jean shorts and a lavender tank top, with a worried expression marring her lovely face. Shoes and sandals from the world's top designers like Prada, Gucci, Jimmy Choo, Louboutin, and Manolo Blahnik among others were scattered across the carpeted floor. Inexplicably, the expansive shoe closet was empty.

Olivia gazed at him with tear glistened eyes. What was going on? The shoe closet was enormous and would easily accommodate all her shoes with room for more.

Sergio kneeled down in front of her, and gently placed his hands on her thighs, her skin soft and warm. His heart melted seeing her so distressed.

"What's the matter? There's more than enough room for your shoes, isn't there?"

Then it hit him like a ton of bricks. Was she reconsidering moving in with him? Had she changed her mind and was hiding in the closet until she worked up the courage to tell him she was leaving before she'd even gotten fully unpacked? Sergio's fingers and toes went numb, and he experienced shortness of breath, making him feel faint.

Olivia squeezed his hands gently. "At my place, although it was spacious, I didn't have this kind of shoe storage. I had most of them labeled in boxes. I'm a little overwhelmed about how to arrange them now that I have all this space."

Thank fuck. He slumped in relief and chuckled. She wasn't leaving. Hadn't changed her mind about moving in.

"I know it seems silly," Olivia said. "I'll figure it out. Did you think I changed my mind about moving in? I haven't, I promise. I *want* to be here with you."

"I admit, you had me worried for a minute." Sergio brought his lips to hers with a light, teasing touch. Olivia's plump, kissable lips tasted like sweet heaven.

She moaned as they shared intense, beautiful kisses. His cock ached to bury itself deep inside her. Mindful of the short amount of time they had, Sergio unceremoniously removed her tank top and unhooked her matching satin lavender bra.

Olivia's nipples puckered, calling out to his lips. He captured one distended tip between his lips, savoring the taste of her heated skin. She arched her back and ran her fingers through his hair.

"We can't right now. We have guests and you're cooking for us."

Sergio smiled at her use of the word "we" and captured her other nipple with his teeth and tugged, causing her to moan.

"We'll have to make this quick then," was Sergio's reply. He unbuckled his cargo shorts and tore off his shirt. "Hurry, take your shorts and panties off."

Olivia awkwardly worked on getting her shorts off while sitting on the couch.

"Hey, guys. Are you in here? Antonella's ready to get the grill going so we can eat."

Shit. It was Elisa. Damn it. "Shhh. Don't say anything." Sergio urged Olivia. They were so close, and he was so hard. Their guests could wait a few minutes, couldn't they?

Unfortunately, Olivia didn't seem to agree, shoved at him, and gathered her clothes. "Yes, we're here. We'll be down in a minute," she called out.

"Fuck. Tell my sister I don't appreciate getting cock blocked in my own home," Sergio said as he grabbed his discarded shirt. He'd figure out a way to get her back.

He heard Elisa snicker, the smart ass. "I'll make sure to mention it."

About an hour later, under the protection of the screened pergola in the courtyard, they were all seated around the table with perfectly grilled steaks, marinated chicken, bacon wrapped asparagus and baked potatoes. They each had an ice-cold Corona to top off the meal. Maybe he'd let Antonella off the hook after all.

Antonella's grin was a mile wide. She lifted her beer bottle. "I love seeing the two of you together again after being apart for so long. To second chances." They all raised their bottles in salute and took a sip. Antonella glanced lovingly at Elisa. "And to new beginnings."

Sergio hoped that meant the ladies had come out. He couldn't imagine hiding who he was from the world. How painful it must have been for them over the last three years. He wondered if his father's attitude had something to do with the girls remaining in the closet to some extent. Damn him.

Olivia's eyes lit up. "Does that mean what I think it means?"

Antonella's expression turned serious. "Yes. Generally speaking. Elisa and I want to get married."

Olivia bounced in her chair, clapping happily. Sergio couldn't be more pleased. He considered Elisa a third sister. She was also a perfect match for Antonella. His stomach churned as he sensed a "but" coming he wouldn't be happy about.

"If it involves Dad, I don't want to hear it." He wasn't going to risk upsetting Olivia on this day of all days. Hell no.

Olivia surprised him and reached over, squeezing his hand gently. "It's fine. We're family, aren't we?" Sergio didn't think he could love the woman any more than he did, but he was still uneasy.

"I'm expecting Dad to become totally unhinged when we tell him the news. And to be honest, things have been steadily going downhill since you left. Many on your management team have left.

Some in other departments too. Fortunately, the team you put together in Colombia hasn't been affected. Yet."

Sergio wasn't surprised. Olivia squeezed his hand again. His signal to keep his mouth shut. *Yes, ma'am.*

"We need to leave too. Your father is decimating Silvia's legacy and we can't stay and watch him slowly destroy everything," Elisa said, her voice devoid of emotion.

"Uncle Emmanuel, Juan, and Francisco won't go against him because Dad's the oldest." Antonella added. She reached to the ground beside her and placed a sketch pad in front of Olivia.

Sergio would love to bring Antonella on at Delcinia. She was an immense talent the company would be lucky to have. Elisa too. Pissing his father off when he found out was an added bonus.

"You're hired. Both of you," Sergio announced with lightness in his chest.

"Absolutely!" Olivia agreed.

Elisa nodded happily, seemingly relieved.

Antonella glared at him. "Can I present my pitch at least?"

Sergio rolled his eyes. "Go ahead." He was certain he and Olivia would love Antonella's ideas. And he was certain that Camille, Isabella and Sienna would welcome her with open arms.

"Since you're expanding into non-lingerie items with the Essence line and offering larger sizes, I got to thinking." Antonella opened the sketch pad and moved it between him and Olivia. "What about expanding Delcinia's product line a little more. I call it the Essentials line."

He and Olivia flipped through the pages. Olivia oohing and aahing at the designs in various shades of purple. Smart, but not necessary. Sergio quickly recognized the potential of the casual dresses in mini, midi, and maxi lengths with assorted necklines. Her designs included rompers, jumpsuits, leggings, and a complete line of sportswear. It was all perfect in his opinion. Antonella had obviously poured her heart out designing everything.

"I love all of this, including Essentials as the line name. Are you *really* sure you want to come work for us? Both of you?" Sergio shared Olivia's concern about his father's reaction to Antonella's and Elisa's desertion from Martinez Designs, but they were grown women and they needed to do what was best for their careers and futures.

Antonella and Elisa both nodded happily. He'd bet they couldn't wait to give notice. Or not. Sergio hadn't bothered to, and his father certainly hadn't deserved the courtesy.

Olivia turned to him with a gleam in her eyes and raised a brow. They'd be idiots to refuse. Good thing he and Olivia weren't idiots. Sergio nodded at his business partner.

"Welcome to you both. There isn't enough time to include any of these designs in the September show, but we can get started planning for next February." Olivia glanced down at the sketch pad and grinned as she continued looking everything over.

"Of course," Antonella said. "If Essentials does well, I was thinking we could add sexy evening dresses and club wear."

Sergio thought that was an excellent idea. Elisa glanced at him with tears in her eyes and mouthed *thank you*. Sergio winked back. He looked forward to having them on board. Sergio anticipated Valeria would probably follow them to Delcinia, and he had no problem with that. In fact, he preferred having them all under one professional roof.

Olivia glanced back up with concern etched on her face. "Carlos is going to be furious. We all know that. But can I ask if he knows I've moved in with Sergio?"

"*I* certainly didn't tell him, and I don't give a shit what he thinks about it if he *does* know." Sergio's father's opinion about his life was irrelevant and unwelcomed.

"Val told him the other day. She was so excited it slipped out," Antonella admitted.

Olivia pursed her lips, seemingly processing the information. "Dare I ask what he said? Not that it matters, but..."

Elisa shrugged. "He didn't really say anything. I was surprised."

Yet. Sergio's father hadn't said anything *yet*. He knew his father well. A storm was brewing, and when Antonella and Elisa came out and then quit, all hell would break loose.

And that's what worried Sergio most. His and Olivia's newfound relationship was still fragile. He couldn't. Wouldn't allow his father to fuck things up for them a second time. Until the inevitable showdown, he'd enjoy his and Olivia's "love bubble," as she referred to it, and pray they survived the aftermath of Carlos Martinez.

Chapter Six

September – New York Fashion Week

Seated at Sergio's conference table in his office at Delcinia's HQ, he and Olivia reviewed the inaugural recipients of the new scholarship program. Award letters had been sent two months ago, and he was incredibly pleased with the program's launch. Sergio wanted to see the program grow so they could help many more girls achieve their dreams. He was incredibly proud of the launch and Olivia for conceptualizing the program.

The girls that had been selected were ambitious, hardworking and deserving. They'd be well received at the big-donor charity ball in two weeks. The attending Darlings, male and female, were enthusiastic to lend their support for the event and the program.

Sergio wanted to do more, however. College wasn't for everyone. He knew this from personal experience with family and friends.

He gazed over at Olivia, who was busy on her laptop and couldn't help but smile. Sergio was so fucking happy he didn't recognize his life sometimes. When she sensed him watching her, she looked up from the screen. Olivia's smile made his heart swell with love. She raised a curious brow.

"What do you think about implementing a paid internship program for girls who might not see college as an option but still want to make a way for themselves? We could start with areas in the design, photography, and marketing departments." Sergio liked the idea even more now that he'd expressed it out loud. Would Olivia? Or would she feel that he was undermining her efforts?

Olivia's jaw dropped. "I love that idea. College isn't for everyone but that doesn't mean you can't have a successful, well-paying career." Her fingers flew over the laptop keyboard, he assumed to make preliminary notes about the program. "We could also include internships in the factories and with the seamstresses."

He hadn't initially considered that, but Sergio was onboard with that idea as well. His concerns about living together while also working together had been quashed. He and Olivia related well regardless of their setting. Period. Even better now than they did when they'd first met ten years ago. Older and wiser, he supposed.

"Since the fall fashion show is in four days, let's take one last look at the Essence line before it goes live on the online store. I think everything looks great. Having the options with the lace detailing turned out so well." An easy smile spread across Olivia's face as they scrolled through the online store photos. The Essence line was going to be a huge success based on the prototype feedback, and adding men's garments had been a brilliant idea.

Their customers were going to flip next February when they introduced Essence jeans to the line. The denim fabric was soft, stretchy, and ultra comfortable. The stylish prototypes for men and women looked and felt like a dream. Olivia had hit a home run with the Essence line.

They moved on to the new additions to the Eden and Enchantment lines. The latest items were beautiful, and Sergio was certain they'd be well received and sell well. The larger Darlings were absolutely gorgeous, and he hoped would expand their customer base to women who couldn't see themselves wearing Delcinia lingerie before.

"Natalie's and Faith's pictures are truly stunning. Faith sure came around, didn't she?" Sergio was proud of Faith. She'd been so shy in the beginning but now exuded confidence he hoped would inspire other women.

Olivia beamed with pride. "I know." She grasped his hand, her eyebrows drawing together with concern. "Vera would have been thrilled with the upcoming show and everything we've accomplished. Has Henry responded to his show invitation?"

Sergio's shoulders drooped and his chest ached. Vera Delair's funeral had taken place two weeks ago. Attended by the who's who in the fashion industry, celebrities, politicians, and former and current Darlings, it had been a celebration of Vera's life, her enduring partnership with Henry and her many accomplishments.

Henry had put on a brave face for everyone, but privately when they were alone, he'd broken down. Sergio, Olivia, and Camille comforted Henry and each other as best as they could. They were all heartbroken. Vera's passing was an enormous loss.

"No reply." Sergio didn't blame him. "I reserved a spot of honor for him beside Allegra if he decides to attend." Attending the show could bring Henry the comfort he so badly needed right now.

Olivia frowned and rubbed her eyes. Between the work she'd done preparing for the upcoming show, the Essence line, planning the first scholarship charity ball, and her modeling obligations, she had to be exhausted.

"Let me take you to the Hamptons for a few days after the charity ball. You need a break, and we have a competent staff in place to take care of things while were gone." Sergio could use a break himself, but he cared more about what Olivia needed. *She* was his priority, first and foremost.

Before she could answer, Sergio heard a commotion in the hallway. "I'm sorry sir, but you need an appointment to see Mr. Martinez," Sergio's executive assistant Ruby said with confidence and authority. Vera and Henry had spoken highly of the capable, no-nonsense, long-time employee who didn't take shit from anyone. Sergio hadn't regretted keeping her on after he'd taken over the company. She had yet to disappoint him and was a valuable asset to the company.

"Mr. Martinez is my *son*, and you can't keep me away from him!"

"If you don't leave immediately, I'm going to call security and the police. I don't care who you are."

Olivia cursed under her breath. Their love bubble had officially popped. Shit. Sergio had known it was only a matter of time, but his father's timing couldn't have been worse. They had so much going on. Multiple balls in the air.

Sergio opened his office door to find Ruby nearly ready to take his father down personally. His lips twitched in amusement. No one messed with Ruby, and his father was about to find out if he didn't calm the hell down.

His father, on the other hand, although his eyes were narrowed and his hands were clenched into fists, seemed haggard. His hair was tousled, his navy suit was wrinkled, and his eyes were red. For a moment, Sergio felt sorry for the man. The feeling passed quickly.

"What the fuck are you doing here?" Sergio didn't have time for his father's bullshit so the faster he could get him to leave, the better.

"I need to speak with you. It's important. *Please*."

The weakness in his father's voice surprised Sergio as well as his use of the word please. Sergio gestured to his office and his father entered, followed by Ruby.

"As an additional witness," Ruby whispered as she walked past Sergio. He chuckled. She was getting a raise. A substantial one.

When his father noticed Olivia sitting at the conference table, he visibly stiffened. "I need to speak with my son alone. Leave us now."

Ruby gasped, but Olivia, with tears glistening, made to stand. Fury burned hot in Sergio's gut.

"Don't fucking move," he blurted to Olivia, not meaning to sound so harsh.

Olivia flinched, her eyes widening.

"I'm sorry. I'd like for you to stay," Sergio said in a calmer, more even tone. He turned to his father and glared. "Don't ever fucking speak to Olivia like that again. Understand? We're partners in *every* way. Say what you have to say and get the hell out of here."

Sergio was stunned when Olivia gestured for his father to sit at the table. She was too decent for the likes of Carlos Martinez. His father sat down and ran a shaky hand through his silver hair. He glanced at Ruby but didn't say a word.

Heaving a sigh, Carlos hung his head. "I need your help. Everything's a mess without you. Before Antonella, Elisa, and Valeria left, many on your management team had already left. Others continue leaving. I can't. I can't run the company."

Sergio took his place at the table beside Olivia. He clasped her hand and gave it an assuring squeeze. She nodded back at him, with a compassionate smile curving her luscious lips. She was too good for the likes of Carlos Martinez.

"No shit." Sergio wouldn't make it easy for his father. Not after all he'd been through because of him. "You made my time at Martinez Designs and my life a living nightmare while I was there. I own my own company now. With Olivia. I've never been happier. Why the hell would I want to help *you*?"

"Because Delcinia is a *family* business, just like Martinez Designs and Wilson Dairy are. And family sticks together. They support each other," Olivia said evenly, squeezing Sergio's hand. His father nodded, wiping tears from his eyes. What the hell was happening?

"Are you suggesting I go back to Martinez Designs?" It was absolutely out of the question. Sergio was never leaving Delcinia or Olivia. Under *any* circumstances. "No fucking way. I'm not leaving you or Delcinia. Ever."

Olivia wore a confident, cocky grin on her beautiful face. "Of course not. What I'm suggesting is Martinez Designs becomes a fully owned subsidiary of Delcinia. We'll put a competent management team back in place. Martinez can offer some of our new Essence line at their stores. We can cross promote the brands and product lines. It can be a fairly seamless transition, *if* you agree."

Fuck. Olivia was right, her plan could work. But did Sergio really want to show his father mercy that he certainly did not deserve?

"And we'd finally get Martinez Designs into the Walhstrom resort and hotel gift shops. I never understood why you wouldn't let them carry inventory." Sergio wasn't fully on board with the idea of an acquisition, but the idea was worth serious contemplation and discussion. "And there are fine points that need to be ironed out first. The most important point is assurance in writing, that you will not interfere in any way with operations. If you do, the company will be put up for sale. Period."

Sergio's father glanced at him, Olivia, and Ruby with gratitude. "Our family came from nothing and built something wonderful. I never wanted the Walhstroms to think I wasn't good enough for Justine, so I didn't accept their charity."

What? Sergio'd had no idea his father had felt inadequate. His father had loved his mother dearly and the Walhstrom family knew it.

Olivia looked Carlos squarely in the eyes. "From what Brooks and Margot told me, the Wahlstroms respected you and what your family accomplished. Charity is charity and business is business. They wanted to carry your designs because they're exceptional, not out of pity. They're going to carry some of our Essence line, and we're thrilled."

Sergio's father nodded. "That's on me then. Another failure for not understanding that. All the more reason for me to hand things over to the both of you and 'stay in my lane,' as Sergio has insisted so many times over the years, but I never listened."

Sergio grunted. "That's an understatement." He was pissed his father had put him in this position. And grateful Olivia had chosen to try to find a reasonable solution rather than leave. He didn't deserve her.

"Will you consider Olivia's acquisition idea? Salvage what I've ruined? Preserve the family's legacy?" Sergio had never experienced his father so agreeable. Hat in hand, heart on his sleeve. It was disconcerting.

"I'll consider it if you agree to all my conditions." Sergio wasn't leaving anything to chance. He wasn't certain his father could be trusted, not after so much had happened. For all Sergio knew, his father's visit could be some sort of trick. He wasn't taking any unnecessary risks.

His father blew out a relieved breath. "Thank you, *hijo*. I promise you won't regret it."

Sergio hoped not. His personal and professional futures were now on the line.

Energy buzzed backstage a few minutes before Delcinia's September fashion week show was due to begin. On time, about twenty minutes late. It was Olivia's last show before transitioning to Honorary Darling status to devote her time to corporate operations. A surreal moment to say the least. But one she eagerly embraced and accepted.

Olivia was kicking off the show in a racy new bra, panty, and garter belt set designed by Sienna Bellucci in Olivia's signature purple. She glanced around the backstage area in awe. Her years of hard work and dreams were all coming to fruition. Olivia's heart was full, and she teared up.

The new male Darlings were hamming it up for the film crew, joined by some of the larger sized female Darlings. Her sisters were enthusiastically chatting with more senior Darlings – all caught by the film crew. It hadn't gone unnoticed to Olivia that her sisters had seemed smitten with two of the male Darlings in particular. She hadn't said anything, yet, but planned to revisit her suspicions soon.

Regardless of possible love connections, Olivia ached with pride. It was going to be their best show to date.

"Everyone. Henry's here." Sergio's father called out to the room in excitement. The room erupted in cheers and applause. "You should do something to honor his attendance. Show respect, don't you agree, *hija*?"

Carlos was now referring to Olivia as daughter. In the four days since his appearance at Delcinia HQ, she, Sergio and Carlos had spent meaningful time together and had come to an agreement about the acquisition. The transaction would close after the fundraiser charity ball. She was cautiously optimistic about their plans.

Father and son were slowly rebuilding their relationship, and she and Carlos were finally getting to know each other like they should have done years ago. Carlos was also mending fences with the

Walhstroms, who had welcomed him with open arms, understanding, and support.

"Why don't the ladies blow Henry a kiss on their first pass by him and the men nod in recognition?" Sergio said, now beside her.

Olivia loved the idea. Everyone, including Carlos murmured and nodded in agreement.

Butterflies danced in Olivia's belly as she took her place behind the curtains as the show was about to begin. Her last Delcinia show as Lead Darling. The end of an era. The beginning of another. Tears threatened, but she held them at bay. Olivia took a deep breath as their announcer began speaking. This was it.

"Welcome everyone. We dedicate today's show to the late Vera Delair. Forever loved. Never forgotten."

Three hours later, Olivia giggled as Sergio fumbled with the hotel room key at the Grand Walhstrom. He'd planned ahead and reserved the same room she'd stayed in when she'd first arrived in New York. The fateful day they met. Who knew Sergio was so sentimental?

The door clicked. "Finally," Sergio growled and pushed it open, gesturing for Olivia to enter.

She was greeted by the soft scent of roses. Stepping farther inside the room, she gasped. Multiple arrangements and bouquets of roses in various shades of purple were placed around the room with petals sprinkled on the bedspread. Champagne was chilling in a silver ice bucket stand with two glasses on the nightstand.

A flash of adrenaline tingled through Olivia and her heartbeat kicked up. It had been such an emotional day. The show had gone extraordinarily well. Their new designs and the Essence line had been a sensation. Henry'd had tears sliding down his face underneath his sunglasses as all the Darlings had paid their respects, and he blew kisses back to them. It had been so touching, she teared up thinking about it.

At the end of the show, Akira nearly fainted when Olivia had announced she was stepping down as Lead Darling and passing the torch to her. She'd accepted a bouquet of red roses graciously, promising to not let the company down. Henry had stayed for the after party, his spirits seemingly lifted, at least for now. It had been a lot to take in, and Olivia now felt overwhelmed.

As if sensing her fragile state, Sergio led Olivia to the bed. She sat on the edge, allowing her pent-up tears to fall. Sergio kneeled down in front of her and clasped her hands.

"*Mi dulce amor.* I know it's been an emotional day. For everyone." He leaned up and brushed his lips lightly against hers.

Olivia nodded, grateful he understood. Sergio patiently provided the time and space she needed to settle down.

"Emotional yes, but a wonderful day nonetheless." Olivia wouldn't have traded a single moment of the day for anything.

"It certainly was." He reached into his suit pants pocket and retrieved a small black velvet box. "I hope to add one last bit of wonder to the day if you think you can handle it."

Fresh tears streamed down Olivia's cheeks and her hands covered her mouth. She trembled, warmth spreading through her.

Sergio opened the box revealing a magnificent cushion shaped lavender diamond, surrounded by white diamond accents with white diamond accents along each side of the band. It was absolutely stunning.

He slipped it on Olivia's ring finger. A perfect fit and dazzling against her skin.

"I've been holding onto this ring since before your twenty-first birthday. Far too long. It's always been yours, just like I have been. You're the only one I've ever loved. I'll never love another.

Marry me, Olivia." Sergio feathered kisses along her knuckles and a spike of heat ricocheted down her spine.

"I've never loved anyone else either. Yes. I'll marry you. Just try to stop me."

A satisfied smirk curved Sergio's lips, and he claimed her mouth in a mind-blowing kiss as he repositioned them onto the bed. Their tongues tangled and tantalized in between fumbling to undress as quickly as they could.

"No. Leave the garter belt and stockings on," Sergio whispered after she'd removed her bra and panties. Olivia had worn the set she'd opened the Delcinia show with.

As if he was famished, Sergio buried his face between her thighs, lapping at her drenched slit and flicking his tongue against her sensitive clit. Olivia's eyes drifted closed, and her body hummed and shook with pleasure.

She felt the weight of her beautiful engagement ring when she ran her fingers through Sergio's thick hair, pulling him closer. His talented tongue lashed and worked her pussy until her whole body shuddered, surrendering in release.

Her eyes flew open when she heard a condom wrapper tear open. Olivia grabbed Sergio's hand before he could sheath his thick erection.

"Don't." Olivia wanted to feel her man without a barrier.

Sergio raised a brow, a devilish grin curling his lips. Olivia nodded and he tossed the condom aside.

He parted her thighs wider, her pussy pulsing for him. Sergio moved the tip of his dick against her, teasing her folds open. Olivia groaned out in delight when he thrust inside with one bold stroke.

Skin to skin with the man she loved with her heart and soul, he fucked her with sure, possessive thrusts, making her feel so cherished and adored tears fell. Sergio rammed in and out of her wet pussy with wild fury, his hips grinding against her, her arms and legs tightly wrapped around him.

They fucked with intense, carnal ferocity as one. Now and forever. Sergio whispered his undying love for her in a rough, urgent voice. Heat consumed her as their bodies continued to grind together.

Pure bliss surged inside her as Olivia flew over the edge. Sergio's body jerked and bucked as he spurted his warm release inside of her.

After a moment, he rolled and lay beside her, holding her now bejeweled hand. "*Cariña*, no condom. What if..."

Olivia placed their joined hands on her chest, her heart beating steadily with love. "I'm on the pill, remember?" They were getting married and would start a family. Hopefully, sooner rather than later so she saw no reason to continue with additional protection.

"The pill isn't foolproof." Sergio countered, though he didn't seem bothered.

"Should – well, would it bother you *if*?" Olivia didn't think so or he would have slipped the condom on before they'd had sex.

"Not at all. I'm looking forward to it. When you're ready."

Olivia was so lucky. Dreams delayed were now coming true, and she was overjoyed.

"I'm relieved my proposal didn't cause more stress after the day you've had. I wanted to propose today because I was there when you first came to New York to begin an exciting new phase of your life. And I'm still here with you now, for the beginning of another."

Sergio was absolutely right. Olivia hadn't considered that. He poured them each a glass of chilled champagne to toast the next phase. When their stomachs growled, he called down for room service. Good thing he knew the people who ran the joint.

Epilogue

5 years later

Seated at a small table in the corner of Wilson Dairy's ice cream shop in Orrville, Ohio, Sergio nearly inhaled his sundae. He couldn't help himself. The superior vanilla ice cream, topped with hot fudge and caramel then covered with roasted pecans, whipped cream and a cherry was so fucking delicious, Sergio considered getting another when he was finished. Henry who sat beside him on the other hand, displayed considerable restraint as he enjoyed his strawberry sundae with couth.

"My God this is good. How do they make the ice cream so rich and creamy?" Henry asked as he finished his treat.

Sergio knew, but couldn't share the Wilson's secrets. Their ice cream was only one part air to every two parts of cream. They used 18% butterfat and only the finest ingredients. It was rich, creamy and made in small batches using cream made from the same milk their farm's cows produced.

"I could tell you, but then I'd have to kill you." Sergio teased.

All kidding aside, Sergio finished his sundae and glanced around the store. Their family had needed a break from their busy lives in New York and visiting the Wilson farm was the perfect way for all of them to slow things down a beat and decompress.

His sister Antonella and her wife Elisa were behind the counter learning how to serve customers by Olivia's sisters Faith and Natalie, while sampling the inventory in the process. As Sergio had expected, his father had been taken aback when the women had come out and quit their jobs at Martinez Designs. But to his surprise, he'd regrouped quickly, perhaps learning his lesson from what had gone down between him and his only son.

He had proudly escorted Antonella down the aisle on her wedding day. Sergio had escorted Elisa as her parents had essentially disowned her. Fortunately, there had been plenty of Elisa's younger and more open-minded family members, including her older sister, who had attended their wedding and supported her.

Sergio turned toward the front of the store when he heard the angelic giggle of his and Olivia's four-year-old daughter Justina. She'd been named after his late mother, and took after Olivia with dark blonde hair and blue eyes. His father wiped her face wearing a huge grin. The two adored each other. His father had asked if he could be the one to teach the girl Spanish. He and Olivia had happily agreed and Justina was already quite fluent. His father had turned out to be a caring and doting grandfather.

His executive assistant Ruby was also seated at the table, enjoying a loaded banana split. No one had seen it coming when she and his father had announced they were in a relationship two years ago. It seemed Ruby, a widow herself, was able to keep his father grounded and in line.

A low growl escaped Sergio's lips as his youngest sister Valeria and her gorgeous three-year-old daughter Luciana joined his father, Ruby and Justina at their table.

"It's been nearly four years. You need to let it go. It's not healthy," Henry said, his tone even and calm.

"Maybe you and Dad should have let me beat the shit out of Diego and I would be."

Henry raised a brow and shook his head. "It would have made things worse and you know it."

Would it have? Sergio wasn't so sure. Beating the crap out of Diego after he'd knocked up his sister and then abandoned her would have made him feel a hell of a lot better.

It had been Sergio's father and Henry who had convinced him to leave the dead beat alone for Valeria's sake. They'd assured him that Valeria would eventually find the love she deserved and a worthy father figure for his precious niece.

"Breaking his nose would have made me feel a lot better."

Henry chuckled. "I don't doubt that, but Valeria's happy. Lucy's thriving. It all worked out in the end. That's what matters. Not Diego. He was a loser from the get go."

Sergio couldn't agree more. He'd never liked Diego. And Henry was right, Valeria and his precious niece were happy. That's all he'd ever wanted for them.

Henry's face lit up when Olivia's Aunt Brenda entered the ice cream shop. An unexpected romance had bloomed and everyone couldn't have been more pleased. Brenda had ended an abusive marriage several years before and had fallen hard for Henry. Henry had been blindsided by their connection, convinced he'd never love another after Vera had passed.

"Vera would approve of Brenda, you know? She'd be happy you've moved on and are happy." Sergio knew Henry sometimes felt guilty about having a new woman in his life.

"I know. She told me many times before she died that she hoped I'd find happiness with another. I'll always love Vera, and miss her. But I thank the heavens above every day for Brenda." Henry nodded and went to join his new lady at the counter where she was placing her order. Sergio was grateful fate had brought the two together. They deserved their happiness.

Joy bubbled up when Sergio's gaze landed on Olivia and their six-month-old Delia, who was sleeping peacefully in Olivia's arms despite the noise and chatter around them. Peace and satisfaction hummed through his veins. They'd had a difficult time conceiving their youngest, but after nearly two years of trying they'd been blessed with their little angel. Sergio had never felt happier or more alive than he did now and was grateful Olivia had given their love a second chance.

Olivia approached Sergio, now sitting alone, with their youngest and another turtle sundae for her husband. Her mother had held Delia for her while she'd enjoyed a scoop of coconut chocolate almond ice cream, one of her favorite flavors.

Their trip to Orrville had been exactly what everyone had needed. As happy as they were in New York, their lives were hectic and demanding. Routine downtime was absolutely necessary and welcomed.

"No dessert after supper for you, Mister." Olivia teased, taking a seat next to Sergio and placing his sundae in front of him.

He dug in, greedily inhaling a huge scoopful. "Yes, ma'am. It's not my fault, though. It's your family's for making such exceptional ice cream."

Olivia didn't disagree. All the dairy's products were of the highest quality and their continued sales growth was proof of that.

She rocked their sleeping baby gently in her arms, grateful for the blessing of Delia. It had been a rough road but worth the stress, tears and time it took to bring her into the world.

Justina waved at her and the baby from her table. Olivia blew her first born a kiss and winked at Carlos. Surprising them all, he'd shown himself to be a caring and patient grandfather to all three of his granddaughters.

Olivia leaned back in her chair, snuggling Delia, basking in the peace flowing through her. Sometimes she didn't believe her life. How different things would have been had she not given Sergio a second chance, not that it mattered now.

She watched as Carlos held court at their table, the ladies seated there engaged and smiling as they chatted up a storm.

Olivia had had her doubts about him in the beginning. They all had.

The acquisition of Martinez Designs had gone fairly smoothly with only a few minor hiccups. And although Carlos had agreed verbally and in writing to "stay in his lane" as conditions of the merger, he did offer a suggestion or two along the way that Delcinia had implemented.

They'd expanded the internship program to include Martinez Designs and offered a field trip to the Bogotá factory for the interns. She and

Sergio had turned the first intern trip into a second honeymoon of sorts, staying behind a few additional days after the students had returned back to New York. The Wahlstrom's had provided comped rooms for everyone at their Bogotá resort and continued to do so for the yearly excursion.

Carlos had been happily welcomed back by the Wahlstroms. Select Martinez Designs clothing was now offered at all Wahlstrom hotels and resorts and sold well. The family had joyfully welcomed Ruby into the fold as well. Olivia couldn't help but feel for Carlos and all the years he'd wasted keeping himself away.

The merger had brought the families together in ways none of them could have anticipated. Although Olivia had been sworn to secrecy, Carlos had shared he intended on proposing to Ruby during their Ohio visit. While an unlikely couple, Carlos and Ruby's relationship worked.

Delia slowly came awake in Olivia's arms, stretching and cooing sweetly. She kissed the top of the baby's head, comforted by her scent. Delia's eyes lit up when she noticed her daddy finishing up his second sundae. An unabashed daddy's girl. No doubt about it.

"Want to come to Daddy and give Mommy a little break, beautiful girl?" Sergio took the baby onto his lap and bounced her gently. He was such an attentive dad. Her girls were lucky to have him. Olivia couldn't help but to want to give Sergio a son, not that he didn't adore the girls. She knew he did.

"I was wondering. What do you think about trying for a boy?" Olivia suggested while Sergio showered Delia's chubby little cheeks with kisses. Her giggles made Olivia's heart swell.

Sergio turned to her, raising a brow. "You want to try again? Considering all the trouble we had conceiving Delia?"

Olivia merely shrugged. She had a secret of her own she'd share with Sergio when they were alone. "You don't want a boy? A little mini-me Sergio?"

Sergio chuckled, sending Delia into a giggling fit. "I love our girls to death, you know that. It's not about wanting or not wanting a boy. It's about your physical and our mental health trying again when we had so much trouble the last time. I adore the family we've made. And even with nannies and house staff, are plates are full."

Valid points, but it was too late. By her estimation, Olivia was about two months along. She'd made an appointment with a competent OB/GYN in town during their visit.

"Are you open to discussing it later? After supper and the girls are down for the night?" She'd been surprised but thrilled when she'd read the results of the home pregnancy test she'd taken just before they'd left for Ohio. She prayed Sergio would be too.

"Of course, querida. I'm open to trying for another if you are, regardless of the gender we're blessed with." Sergio leaned closer and sealed the deal with a light kiss.

Thankful he'd most likely not be upset by her news, Olivia sat back and relaxed. She'd been on partial bed rest while carrying Delia, but she felt strong and was hopeful for the possibilities that lay ahead for them.

The End

Are you curious to find out what happened with Valeria and little Luciana? Did things really work out in the end? Pick up a copy of *Passion and Pearls* today at

https://books2read.com/PassionAndPearls and find out!

Stay current with everything Delcinia at the Delcinia Diaries series page at

https://books.bookfunnel.com/DelciniaDiaries

Browse all of Dania's titles at

https://books2read.com/daniavoss/

About the Author

Int'l bestseller and award-winning author Dania Voss writes compelling, sexy romance with personality, heat, and heart. Born in Rome, Italy and raised in Chicagoland, she creates stories with authentic, engaging characters. She loves anything pink and is a huge fan of 80s hair bands.

A favorite with romance readers, her debut novel "On the Ropes," the first in her Windy City Nights series, became an international bestseller. Dania's books have won multiple awards, and her work has been highlighted on NBC, ABC, CBS, and FOX. She has been featured in the Chicago Tribune, Southern Writers Magazine, and Chicago Entrepreneurs Magazine (selected as the #8 Top Chicago Author in 2021).

When she's not writing, you can find Dania at a sporting event, a rock concert, or the movies (preferably a comedy).

Learn more about Dania, her books, and all the ways to follow her, at her website: https://www.daniavoss.com